PROLOGUE

F *UCK.*
How has my life come to this?
My heart raced in my chest and dizziness threatened to consume me as my gaze skittered over the gravel of the bar car park where I sat in the dark, taking in Rob's lifeless body and my torn panties. A sharp chill hit me and although the night was warm, a shiver ran through my body. I pulled my arms around me, trying desperately to push away the ugly thoughts assaulting my mind.

My dress being ripped.

My hair being yanked.

His hands on my body.

His knife slicing my arm.

Bile rose in my throat and I lurched forward. My hands skimmed across the gravel as I tried to stop myself from falling face first onto the ground. Swallowing hard, I glanced up at J who was pacing back and forth, on his phone. His nostrils flared as he snapped something into the phone and his arms swept wide, gesturing wildly throughout the conversation. When he ended the call, he raked his fingers through his hair and blew out a harsh breath.

Crouching in front of me, he said, "Scott will be here soon." His eyes searched mine, looking for what, I wasn't sure. They were so hard, though. Not like the J I knew and loved.

Blinking, I tried to wipe away the tears streaming down my face. And then my eyes slid to Rob's body, sprawled dead on the gravel close by.

You motherfucker. Why did you have to do what you did?

I didn't know how long I sat there like that, staring vacantly at him, but movement to my left caught my attention and I turned to see what it was.

Scott strode towards me, his shoulders pushed back, brows furrowed and lips pressed together. When he reached me, he knelt down and gently touched my arm. "Madison, it's time to go," he said quietly.

I stared into his eyes, not sure what I would find there, but all I saw was tenderness. Unusual. Scott didn't do tenderness. Not very often.

J knelt on the other side of me. "Come on, baby," he said as he tried to help me up.

Pain shot through my body as I stood. I winced but didn't let it slow me. J wrapped his arms around me and helped me to Scott's Charger. I looked back at Rob, my eyes taking in his bloody body and then scanning the area to note my underwear on the ground; a reminder of the attack that had occurred.

J settled me in the back of Scott's car and wrapped a towel around my arm, covering the blood. His blue eyes met mine, full of concern. "Will you be all right here while Scott and I deal with the body?" he asked.

I nodded and he left me; left me to go deal with a body like it was just another thing to do in his day. Well, I guessed it sometimes was. All part and parcel of being a member of the Storm MC. My dad's club. The club I grew up around.

Fuck.

I asked myself again.

How has my life come to this?

1

<hr>

Madison

"Jesus, darlin', you know how to suck, don't you?" the guy whose cock was currently in my mouth said. His hand was on my head trying to direct me, but I didn't need it. Like he said, I had talents. I kept on sucking while my hands reached under to massage his balls, and he groaned with pleasure.

We were in his bedroom, him leaning against a wall with me on my knees. Two hours ago we'd never met and less than two hours from now would be the last he'd ever see of me. This was perhaps a shame because he was one hot guy; built with muscles that screamed to be touched, ink that begged to be traced and a face that any woman would kill to kiss. But I didn't do relationships, not anymore.

I stopped sucking his cock and moved my mouth to lay

kisses up his stomach as I stood, licking and nipping as I went. He was naked and I really just wanted to devour his body – he was that gorgeous. I made it all the way up to his mouth and stood face to face, taking in his grin and his dancing eyes.

He wrapped his arms around me, gripping my ass. "Darlin', I've gotta get these clothes off you and sink my dick into that wet pussy of yours."

Trailing a finger across his lips, I nodded. "Yeah, you do."

Not needing any further encouragement, he lifted my top over my head and discarded it. He repeated these motions with my bra, jeans and panties until I was naked too. His eyes slowly roamed my body, taking it all in until they settled on my face, and he grinned at me again. "Fuck, how many hours do you dedicate to this body to get it lookin' this good?"

Reaching out to hook my finger under his chin so I could pull his mouth to mine, I replied, "I like to fuck my way to this body, baby, so I'd say not enough hours. I'd definitely like to spend more time on it."

It's the one thing that chases away thoughts of everything I gave up years ago.

It's the one thing that makes me feel alive.

Our mouths met and an explosion of sensations shot through me as our tongues and lips tangled. He pulled me close so his erection pressed against my pussy.

Yes.

I ground myself against him so his cock touched my clit. Needing more friction there, I reached down and rubbed myself with his cock while I grabbed his balls with my other hand, rolling them back and forth.

Oh, God, I never want this to end.

His need for me.

My need for him.

So damn good.

These moments were what I craved.

It was in these moments when I felt good that hope flared deep in my soul – that long discarded sense that maybe – *just maybe* – my life could be good again, and I could have love, and passion, and a future with someone.

"Talented with your hands as well, I see," he murmured between kisses.

I bit his lip softly, and then a little harder. "I'm a woman of many talents."

He trailed his tongue down my neck and chest until he took a nipple in his mouth and sucked it, one hand moving to cup my breast as he did so. I threw my head back and enjoyed the pleasure traveling along my skin. I really was a tit girl and couldn't get enough.

"You like that, darlin'?" My moan was enough of an answer.

I tangled my fingers in his hair and applied a little pressure to keep his head and mouth in place, on my breast. Dividing his attention between both my breasts, him sucking on me while I rubbed his cock against my clit was my version of heaven.

Eventually he stopped and moved his mouth to my ear, nibbling on it and then he breathed out, "I'm gonna fuck you now. That okay with you?"

Pleasure had wound itself through my body to the

point where I was more than ready for what he wanted - more than ready for the release it would give me. *The escape I need.* "That's more than okay with me."

He turned us so I was now the one against the wall and reached his hand down to my pussy. I moaned loudly when he pushed two fingers inside me and massaged my walls. "Don't get me wrong, that feels good, but I need your cock, baby," I almost begged.

He smirked and withdrew his fingers. "Hang on, gotta get a condom." He left me for a minute while he located one. I breathed a sigh of relief when I heard the foil packet and saw him put the condom on.

Yes.

Coming back to me, he bent so his face was in my pussy and I screamed out when he licked along my wet folds and dipped his tongue into me. *God damn, that feels so good.* Swirling his tongue inside, he gripped my ass and massaged my cheeks.

My mind duelled with itself; on one hand, I wanted him to continue to tongue fuck me, but on the other hand, I really wanted his cock. In the end, the desire for cock won and I reached down and pulled his mouth away from my pussy. He knew what I wanted and stood up, lifting me as he went. I wrapped my legs around him and I clenched in anticipation.

His cock hit my entrance and he thrust in, hard and fast. Just how I liked it. My arms were around him and I gripped as he thrust in and out, in and out. The pleasure inside me built as we continued our climb. Silence surrounded us except for the grunts and groans as we fought for our release, which was perfect – the less talk, the better. I just needed his body and his time, nothing else. His cock filled me, the friction divine, and when his finger hit my clit to massage it, I went over the edge. I screamed as I came and he grunted in approval. A moment later, his body shuddered as he found his release. We then clung to each other as waves of pleasure flowed through us.

He lifted his head to look at me. "You done, darlin'?"

I nodded and smiled. "Yeah."

He let me down and I headed for his bathroom to clean myself up, grabbing my clothes on the way. Neither of us said a word, but really, what was there to say? We'd both gotten what we wanted.

I locked myself in his bathroom and splashed water on my face, enjoying the cold, cleansing sensation. Turning the tap off, I looked in the mirror. My face had that just-fucked flush and my long brunette hair was a tangled mess. The lipstick I'd applied before hitting the club was long gone and sweat had smudged my makeup. But the thing that stood out the most to me was the dullness I saw in my eyes; the indifference I felt towards life.

The only thing that gave me a buzz anymore was sex, and even that was starting to lose its magic.

2

MADISON

FIFTEEN MINUTES LATER I was on my way home when my phone rang. Retrieving it from my bag, I checked the caller ID. Private number. No way, buddy. I ignored it and threw it back in my bag. However, the asshole was persistent and rang again. I ignored it again but after three more rounds, I was pissed off.

I stabbed at the phone to answer it and snapped, "This had better be good."

"Madison, it's Griff. Got some news for you that you're not gonna like very much."

Fuck. Griff was a member of Storm, the motorcycle club that my Dad was President of, and my brother, Scott, was Vice President of. I grew up in the club; it was my family. However, two years earlier I walked away from that life, moving from Brisbane to Coffs Harbour to put distance between us. Now I spent my time trying to keep my nose out of club business. My family had supported my move two years ago, but they wanted me to come home. Scott often called and visited, trying to convince me, but I never caved. When I left, I'd been a broken mess, and I was still trying to put myself back together. Going home would be going backwards as far as I was concerned.

I sighed. "What's up, Griff?"

"Scott wants you back here. There's some shit going down with Black Deeds and he doesn't want you alone in case they retaliate by going after you."

Black Deeds MC was a rival club Storm often had problems with, so I couldn't see that this would be any different. "Griff, I'm fine, and you can tell Scott I'm not coming back."

"It's bad shit, babe. Be best if you did come home."

"The answer's no. Not happening." I raked my fingers through my hair and blew out a long breath, wishing he would accept my answer and let me get on with my night.

There was a long pause while he took in what I said. He probably hated this part of the job. Dealing with me. I would. "Right. I'll pass that on to Scott," he replied, and then hung up.

I stared at the phone. He gave in way too easily and it made me suspicious. They had to have an agenda and I wondered what would be the next step now that I'd said no. Storm didn't take no for an answer. Ever. And they didn't tend to get caught up in bad situations for too long. They barrelled through anything that got in their way. They had a reputation for being a strong and ruthless club, so there was only one question on my mind. *What the fuck have they gotten themselves into that's made them feel this threatened?*

"Hey, honey, I'm home," I yelled out as I came through the front door.

"I'm in the kitchen, chica," came the reply, and I headed towards the voice.

The scene that greeted me in the kitchen left me stunned. My best friend and roommate, Serena, had filled the kitchen with muffins. It was after midnight and there she was with about fifty muffins spread from one end of the kitchen to the other. Her hair, face and clothes were covered in flour, and there were ingredients and cooking utensils everywhere. Unusual for Serena; my BFF was no domestic goddess.

"What is all this cooking in aid of?" I asked, because it had to be for a reason. Serena didn't often bake.

"My mother," she said simply. And that said it all. Serena's mother was a domineering woman and when she said jump, you said how high.

"Ah, another one of her charity assignments?" Her mother was always doing stuff for charities so I guessed this was just another one of those. Usually, she didn't get Serena to bake though, because let's face it, we all knew her skills in this department were somewhat lacking.

Serena nodded. "Yep, and at the rate I'm going, I doubt she'll ever ask me to cook for her again."

I laughed. "Do you want some help, honey?"

She flashed me a huge grin. "I thought you'd never ask."

We spent the next hour tidying up and getting the muffins packed and ready to be delivered to her mother later that day. At about two a.m. I crawled into bed, exhausted after a long day, but sleep eluded me. Thoughts of Storm and my life before I left assaulted me, and as much as I tried to avoid them, I couldn't.

I'd been in a living hell for most of the year prior to leaving Brisbane. To be honest, it began before that. It started after Rob attacked me which was almost two years before I left, back when I was dating J, the guy who I thought would be my forever. Our relationship had never been the same after J killed Rob when he attacked me. J blamed himself for the attack and I blamed myself for J killing him.

That night had started like any other for me. I'd gone to work at Hyde's, a local bar. Rob worked with me as a bartender and we'd had a fun night with all the regulars. However, after close, while I was waiting for J to pick me up, Rob had turned on me and attempted to rape me in the car park outside the bar. J was late picking me up and arrived mid attack, just as Rob had pulled a knife on me and slashed my arm. Five minutes later, Rob was dead after J shot him and so began our descent into hell.

J and I had been together for a little over two years at that point. We'd been great friends for a lot longer than that. He'd joined Storm when he was nineteen. I was a seventeen-year–old schoolgirl at the time and fell hard for him. However, nothing but flirting happened between us for six years, and during that time, we built a strong friendship. Our relationship as a couple had been fiery. We couldn't get enough of each other, but at the same time, we argued constantly. Our main problem stemmed from the club. J didn't involve me in club business, annoying the hell out of me. I wanted to be a part of every aspect of his life and when he refused to talk about the club with me, I felt closed off from part of him, which led to many arguments.

In the end though, what tore us apart was our inability to deal with the fallout from Rob's death. After the attempted rape, J tried to wrap me in cotton wool. He constantly monitored my whereabouts and tried to dictate where I could go and what I could do. I was not a woman who could cope with that style of relationship. On top of that, I'd started drinking heavily. Feeling responsible for Rob's death and being unable to work through my feelings associated with that, I'd resorted to shutting it all out by hitting the bar.

It started out as a bit of fun, but quickly spiralled into an addiction I couldn't get under control. J had lived with an alcoholic parent and had no tolerance for drinking to excess. He tried desperately to get me help but I blocked all his attempts. This went on for almost a year and the final nail in our coffin had been Jodie, a club whore who J had supposedly cheated on me with. I'd believed the rumours, or perhaps I had wanted to, simply to have an excuse to walk away from the hard work our relationship had become. Sometimes it didn't seem like love was enough when everything else was a struggle.

The year after I left J was the lowest point in my life. My drinking was worse. I had shut myself off from family and friends, and I had hooked up with a violent and controlling biker from Storm's rival club, Black Deeds. Nix was the VP of Black Deeds and getting involved with him had angered my father, brother and J. This had been a good reason for me to continue the relationship because at the time, they were all pissing me off and it felt good to return the gesture. A couple of months into the relationship, I discovered that J hadn't cheated on me. I was gutted that I'd thrown our relationship away so easily because of a lie, and went to him to apologise for not believing in him. That had been a turning point for me because we rekindled our friendship and he tried to help me get my life back on track. The problem was that Nix wasn't about to give me up that easily. Although we had only been together for a very short time, he was committed to keeping us together. He didn't like my friendship with J and the day he worked out I was still in love with him was the day he almost beat me to death. That was the day my life turned in a new direction and led me to where I was now.

I hadn't spoken to J in over two years. I'd also stayed sober in that time. Moving away from Storm saved my life. The problem was, I felt dead on the inside. I was a twenty-nine year old single woman just going through the motions of life. Sure, I had a job, good friends, and a great social life. On the outside, my life looked like fun. But it wasn't real. And I didn't know how to make it any better.

3

MADISON

"HELLO, MY NAME is Madison, and I'm an alcoholic."

"Hello, Madison," the group responded and I proceeded to share my story. This group was my safe place and at that moment I needed them in a way I hadn't for a very long time. As I finished, I blew out my breath and let the group's acceptance and support envelope me. It seeped into my bones as I glanced around the room, offering a small smile in thanks. Someone else started sharing their story and I sat back and silently lent my support, as had been done for me.

When I first started coming to the group two years earlier, I absolutely hated it. Although I knew I had to get my shit together, the last thing I wanted to do was give up drinking. It was the shield I used to stop the grime of life from touching me. When I drank, I could just let it pass on by. In the end, however, it sent me to a place I never wanted to go back to. I may have fought this group and what it offered for a while, but I made myself a promise to clean up my act, and I followed through on this. Slowly, I realised the support I found in the group was exactly what I needed.

I attended meetings weekly. Not so much because I still craved alcohol, because I didn't. No, it was more out of habit and to make sure I never went there again. As I looked around the room, I saw people at varying stages of their journey. The ones I liked to focus on were the AA newbies. They reminded me of how far I'd come and how much stronger I was..

That night, though, I was feeling a little vulnerable. Thinking about Storm and J stirred up old feelings of hurt and anger, feelings I'd spent the last couple of years avoiding. In order to move on, I'd needed to lock away all thoughts of J. I hadn't allowed myself to think about him and that had worked for me, but it wasn't working so well after receiving the call from Griff. And while I didn't feel like a drink, I knew myself enough to know I needed to be at the meeting.

The meeting ended soon after and I headed straight out rather than staying for a coffee. Stepping out into the warm January night, I lit a cigarette as I walked home. My mind moved on to the long list of jobs I had to get done that night. Christ, I was supposed to call my brother over an hour ago. I pulled my phone out and dialled him. No answer. *Fuck.* He would be pissed at me. I left a message and then sent a text to Serena, to let her know I was on my way home.

Me: On my way, what's for dinner?

Serena: Fuck off. You're taking me out.

Me: Am I? Make sure you wear that slutty dress for me.

Serena: Oh, I'll wear it babe but I'm not putting out.

God, how I loved this chick. She was my sunshine at the end of a shitty day. Even on days when I was exhausted, she managed to pick me up. I would forever be thankful for the day she came into my life. When I moved to Coffs Harbour I hadn't expected to find a new family, but that was just what I did find. I'd started a job in a clothing boutique and Serena was my workmate. We'd hit it off straight away. We shared the same sense of humour, and bonded over our love for slutty dresses, heels and inked men. Serena introduced me to her inner circle of friends and I became fast friends with them as well. The five of us were inseparable and they were always there for me.

My phone rang and I answered it, without looking at the caller ID, with some attitude, figuring it was my brother calling back. "Scott, what the fuck is so urgent that you felt the need to leave five shitty messages for me?"

A chuckle came down the line. "Babe, you've got the wrong man."

"Oh, shit. Sorry, Blake, I thought you were Scott. Thank God, it's you." I breathed a sigh of relief.

"Obviously. What have you done to piss him off?"

"Nothing. You know what Scott's like. Always finding something to be pissy about," I snapped. Jesus, just thinking about my brother gave me the shits.

"Babe." Blake paused and I was sure I could actually

hear his mind ticking over. "The words pissy and Scott Cole do not go together in the same sentence. Your brother is far too intense that pissy just doesn't cover it."

I blew out a long, frustrated breath. "Yeah, you're right about that." Blake had met Scott a couple of times, so he'd seen firsthand just how intense my brother could be. "Why are you calling me?"

"Gina told me what a shit day you had so I've made you dinner. Bring Serena too."

"You're a superstar, Blake Stone. We'll be there in about half an hour."

"See you then," he said and we hung up. My day had just gotten better. It was funny how the simple things that friends did could mean so much.

TWO HOURS later I was at Blake's house when my brother finally returned my call.

"Scott," I answered and mentally banged my head against the wall. I really didn't want to deal with his shit.

"You been updated?" Yep, he was pissed at me.

I sighed. "Yeah, Griff called." I hesitated and then threw caution to the wind. "Scott, I don't need or even want to be kept in the loop on this shit." As I held my breath and waited for what I knew would not be a pretty reply, I couldn't help but think of the irony in this situation. Years ago I'd begged J to talk to me about club business and now I wanted nothing more than to be kept out of the loop.

"Fuck, Madison! You got no choice. The club needs to make sure you're safe, so you need to fuckin' wise up and take this shit in."

"What part of 'I'm out' don't you understand?" I rubbed my eyes. It was too late for this argument.

"What part of 'you are never out' do *you* not fuckin' understand?" he snapped back.

I knew I was testing my brother's patience but I gave up caring about that a long time ago. I sat silently, trying to process everything he said.

"Why do we have to rehash this crap every time you decide I should come back?" I searched for Blake's eyes and found them focused on me. He gave me a tight smile and I shook my head back at him. This stuff between Scott and me never got any easier, and Blake knew how hard it was for me.

Scott softened his tone. "Madison, it's different this time. Nix is involved."

A chill ran along my spine at the mention of that name. I sighed again, resigned. "Okay, talk to me."

"Nix has made threats against the club so Dad wants you to leave Coffs Harbour. Move back here, where we can protect you." Scott finally got to the reason for the call.

"No." There was no way I was moving back.

"Why the fuck do you have to be so fuckin' stubborn about this?" Scott's anger filtered through the phone again and I imagined him pacing and getting ready to punch something.

"Scott, you know what I left. I can't come back," I pleaded. I walked out onto the balcony, lit a cigarette and took a long drag. Scott had stopped talking and I hoped he was remembering the mess I was when I left.

"Okay." He blew out a long breath. "But I'm putting a guy on you."

This was not what I wanted but I knew better than to argue. It was Scott's version of a compromise, and as he was not known for compromising, *ever*, I was grateful.

THE NEXT MORNING I woke up with an uneasy feeling in my gut, wondering where all this shit with the club would end up. Making a coffee, I took it into the bathroom with me. Not being a morning person, I needed a caffeine hit to get me going. Serena, on the other hand, was always up at five a.m. to get her run in before work. I didn't understand this current trend for running and really couldn't comprehend anyone wanting to get up that early to do it. Taking my shower, I heard her crashing around in the kitchen making breakfast. I cringed at the thought of the mess she would create making one of her juices; a mess I would have to clean up.

"Maddy, do you want me to make you some breakfast?" she yelled out.

"No, honey, but thanks. I'm just going to grab something on the way."

"Okay," she replied and I smiled to myself. She might struggle in the domestic department but at least she tried. There was no doubt she loved taking care of those she loved.

I finished my shower and took some time to blow-dry my hair and fix my makeup. Normally I didn't spend a lot of time on this for work, but I was feeling down, and on down days, I liked to look my best. I looked in the mirror and didn't mind what I saw. Even though I had done some hard living, I'd come through pretty much unscathed. Since giving up alcohol, I made an effort to live healthily and I was fit and strong thanks to yoga and walking. Inked images and words holding significance to the highs and lows of my life painted some of the skin on my arms and back. However, the most prominent reminder of the shit I'd done in my life was the long scar Rob inflicted on me; it glared at me every damn day, but I didn't begrudge it. Whenever Serena or Blake suggested I ink over it, I always said no. I needed to see it to keep me focused on a path that would take me far away from where I once was.

"I'm ready," I announced as I headed into the kitchen to grab my lunch out of the fridge. Serena and I had a shift together later that day, which I looked forward to.

"Let me just put my hair up and then we can go," she replied and slapped my ass on her way out of the kitchen.

I laughed and shook my head at her. Yep, it was going to be a good day.

Five minutes later, Serena reappeared with her hair done. She tilted her head and smiled at me. I knew she was sussing out my mental state because this was something she often did. "How you doing, chica?" she finally asked.

"I'm not sure," I answered honestly. "The fact that Nix is involved in all of this worries me. Scott didn't give me a lot of info to go on but I can only imagine it is bad. Nix is a motherfucker you don't want to mess with."

Serena nodded. "Yeah, I've worked that out from some of the stuff you've told me in the past. How the hell did you end up dating him?"

I sighed, wishing my naivety and immaturity hadn't led me to make the decisions I had. But no amount of wishing could change my past. "I was so messed up and pissed off with J, and Nix was just there one night. It seemed like a good idea at the time. Dad and I weren't really speaking and I was annoyed at him too. I knew that being with Nix would shit him. I think I kinda did it to get back at all of them; J, Dad and Scott."

This was the most I had spoken about my relationship with Nix to Serena, and she encouraged me to keep sharing. "So you hooked up with him and then kept seeing him?"

"Yeah, he was really into it. Me, not so much, but it had been six months since I broke up with J and I was lonely. I was drinking pretty heavily by then and Nix was the only one who didn't give me grief for it." I shook my head as the memories came flooding back. "When I was drinking, I was a lot easier to boss around. That's probably why he liked me drinking. I just didn't give enough of a shit about anything and went along with whatever he wanted."

Serena moved closer to me and touched me gently on the arm, on my scar. "Did Nix do this to you?"

"No." Shit, this conversation was making me feel ill. The familiar feelings of self-hatred washed over me. Tingles spread through to my hands and the ends of my fingers and my head began to spin. Nausea took hold of my stomach and I actually thought I might vomit. No-one, besides J and Scott, knew how I got my scar and it was something I never wanted Serena or anyone else to find out.

"Hey, honey, are you okay?" Serena sensed my distress and directed me to sit on the couch. She ran into the kitchen and returned with a glass of water, which I took gratefully from her.

I downed the water in one go and focused on my breathing. Serena sat beside me, rubbing my back, providing me with her warmth and comfort. I knew she was worried but I didn't have it in me yet to ease her concerns. All I could think about was that my past was finally going to catch up with me. Fuck Nix. Why did he have to come back into my life? He wasn't the reason for all the crap that took place, but he was the climax to it all. And now he was going to be the catalyst for it all flaring up again.

Serena checked her watch. "We should probably get to work; otherwise, Gina will be in a foul mood with us all day for being late."

I looked at her and nodded, offering a small smile. "Thanks," I whispered, grateful that she knew I needed this conversation to be over.

∼

"Oh, God, these shoes are killing my feet," Serena complained as she fell onto the couch and ripped off her shoes.

It had been a long day, and the heels we wore to work

didn't help. But hell, they looked good and sometimes that was what a girl needed to get her through the day.

It was Friday night and we both had the weekend off. Blake had rounded everyone up to visit his restaurant, Scarlett, for dinner tonight, while Saturday was gearing up to be a girls' day out shopping. Sunday was still open for discussion, but I was hoping for some time in the sun.

"What time did Blake say dinner was?" Serena asked.

"Eight o'clock," I answered and pulled my phone out to see if I had any messages.

"I'm going to take a shower unless you want to go first."

I waved her away after discovering a message from Scott. "You go first. I've got a message from Scott to check." She left me as I began reading.

Scott: *Will you be home tonight?*

Me: No.

Scott: *Text me the address of where you'll be. I've got a guy on the way.*

Me: You're kidding, right? I'm fine tonight, send him tomorrow.

My phone rang and I rolled my eyes when I saw it was Scott. Answering the phone, I spoke immediately, "I'm with friends tonight, Scott. They'll look out for me."

"Madison, just give me the goddamn address. He'll be there in a couple of hours," he snapped.

I huffed out a sigh. "Fine." I reeled off the restaurant's address.

I heard him repeat it to someone in the background and then he ended our conversation with, "I'll be there towards the end of next week to try to talk some sense into you," before he hung up.

I threw my phone on the couch and stomped into my bedroom, frustrated as hell. Despite my snark at my brother, I was grateful he looked out for me, even though my stubbornness had a hard time admitting it aloud. In truth, I hated it, hated the situation Nix was putting me in. Once more, my life seemed close to being controlled. I'd left my family to take ownership of my life, my decisions, and it seemed Nix was preventing that from happening by forcing my family's hand. I just hoped Scott sent one of the prospects; they were a lot easier to boss around.

FAITH THREW her head back and laughed so loud that pretty much all eyes in the restaurant were on us. She had a pretty wicked sense of humour and when she found something funny, everyone knew it. Rowan had just relayed a story about something that happened to him at work and although it was kind of funny, Faith thought it was hilarious. It amazed me that these two used to date a couple of years back and had managed to stay friends after they broke up. In fact, from what I'd been told, they were better friends now than when they dated. I never managed to stay friends with any of my exes.

Rowan leaned across the table and touched my hand. "You're quiet tonight." His voice was low so the rest of the group, who kept bantering back and forth, wouldn't hear. Rowan was one of the most sensitive guys I'd ever met.

Serena had introduced us at a party where I knew no-one and he'd gone out of his way to stay close to me that night to make sure I was okay. He was also the guy who would bring you soup and medication when you had the flu and the guy who gave up his plans to go to a football game when you needed someone to go with you to visit your sick grandfather. Yep, he had done those things for me as well as so much more. He was also one of the hottest guys I'd ever met – tall, really well built, covered in ink and bald. However, neither of us were interested in anything more and I valued his friendship.

"Yeah, there's some stuff going down with Scott and the club. He's trying to get me to go back home again," I replied.

"And you're refusing again?" He grinned and shook his head. Rowan and I had often discussed my brother's desire for me to return home, and because he had sisters, he was sympathetic towards Scott.

"Of course I am. So now he's sending someone here to look out for me." I sighed.

Rowan laughed. "You would drive me fucking insane if you were my sister, Madison. I can just imagine the hell you're going to give this poor guy."

At that exact moment, I glimpsed him entering the restaurant, the guy who Scott sent. And I couldn't believe my eyes. Over six foot of pure muscle, tanned and inked skin, dark hair and piercing blue eyes, he was as gorgeous today as the last time I saw him. My heart beat faster and I blocked everything else out as my mind focused on the man heading straight for me. He looked as pissed as I was.

Yeah, I bet he didn't want this gig and I could picture the battle he probably had with Scott about it.

I pushed my chair back and stood, ready to face him. It had been two years since we'd seen each other and while my head was screaming that it didn't want to see him, my body betrayed me. I had that fluttery feeling in my stomach; felt that familiar need, deep in my core. No man had ever affected me like he did.

Walking up to me, he ignored everyone around us. "Madison."

His gravelly voice did me in; it always had. Weak at the knees, I gripped the chair to steady myself; there was no way he would see me falter. He'd sent me away two years ago, ripped my heart out and crushed it, and I would be damned if he discovered what he was still capable of doing to me. Lifting my face, I met his eyes. "J."

4

JASON

FUCK, SHE WASN'T going to make this easy for either of us. I was convinced Scott was handing me my balls on a plate by sending me to her. One look at Madison and I wanted to shove them at her and get the fuck out of there. Christ, she was still as goddamn sexy as the last time I laid eyes on her. I ran my eyes down her body and took in the low-cut, short dress and fuck-me heels. God, I loved those shoes and my dick twitched just thinking about wrapping those legs around me.

"Can we talk outside for a minute?" I asked.

She pursed her lips and appeared to be assessing the situation before she gave me a curt nod and said, "Fine." And with that, she grabbed her purse, brushed past me and stalked towards the front door. I watched her ass sway as I followed her out and told my dick to settle the fuck down.

No way were we going there again. I was there for one reason and one reason only.

Once outside, she reached into her purse and pulled out a cigarette. She quickly lit it and took a long drag. God, I hoped she was still sober. Last I'd heard, she was and she looked pretty healthy, but the way she sucked on that cigarette looked like a junkie fixing for their next hit.

"Scott told you I was coming, yeah?" I asked, taking in the glare she levelled on me. Yep, balls on a plate.

"No," she snapped. "He said someone was coming but he failed to mention it was you." She looked like she was going to say something else but took another long drag on her cigarette instead.

"Well, you've got me until he pulls me back home, so I say we make the best of a shitty situation and put our crap aside."

She took another long drag on her cigarette, threw it down and ground it out before scowling at me. "Go to hell, J. In fact, go home and tell Scott to send someone else. You and I have too much between us. This will go a lot smoother for everyone if he sends another guy."

It was time to take my balls back. Scott had pissed me off by forcing me to babysit, and in less than two minutes Madison was already irritating the fuck out of me. "Babe, sending me away and waiting for someone else to turn up leaves you by yourself. Trust me when I say you do not want Nix to find you alone."

"Don't call me babe," she started and then stopped, as if she'd been about to say something else before hesitating. Her hand moved to rub the scar I knew was on her arm and she blinked a few times before continuing. "I really don't think Nix is going to come here looking for me. Scott's overreacting."

I shook my head. "You've got no idea, Madison. The Nix you knew two years ago has nothing on who he is now. Since he became President of Black Deeds, he wouldn't think twice about fucking over his own mother, let alone you."

"I know what that motherfucker is capable of. I *know* what he can do." She moved close and jabbed a finger in my chest.

Anger swirled around us, threatening to snap my patience. I flicked my hand out and grabbed her wrist, startling her. I made a quick decision to shock her into understanding just what Nix did to those in his way. Grabbing my phone out with my free hand, I scrolled to a photo and shoved it in her face. "Yeah, babe, I know what he did to you, but this...this is what he did to Bec."

Her face paled and I let her rip her hand away from mine. A fraction of a second later, her open palm hit my cheek, which I should have been ready for, knowing her preference for doing that when she was pissed at me. Anger burned through me, not just at her slap but at this whole fucked-up situation. Allowing my anger to lead, I shoved her up against the wall behind her, keeping one hand on her waist and one on the wall above her head. "Listen the fuck up 'cause I'm not going to repeat myself. Nix is out for blood and I'm betting he hasn't let go of the shit that went down between you two. He wasn't ready to let you go, Madison, and nobody walks away from him like you did. Bec tried, and what you saw in that picture is what he did to her. You want that to happen to you?"

Staring at me with eyes wide, her expression blanched. "They were together? And he killed her for leaving?"

I loosened my hold on her and stepped back to give her some space. "Now we're getting somewhere. Yes, from what we've heard he raped her, let his guys take a go as well, and then slit her throat. They dumped her body outside our clubhouse."

Madison's hand flew to her mouth and she released a sob. Fuck, I hadn't wanted to tell her the details, but she'd left me no choice. I knew shocking her into allowing me to stay was the only way she would cave. Tears streaming down her face, I pulled her close to comfort her. I was surprised as shit when her arms wrapped around me, but I hugged her back in silent support. We stayed like that for about five minutes and it felt good to have her in my arms again, but I knew once she pulled herself together, she'd push me away. Fuck, she'd probably slap me again.

We were interrupted by the ringing of my phone. Madison pulled away, wiped her eyes and reached in her purse for a tissue. I focused my gaze on her as I answered my phone. "Yeah?"

It was Scott. "You got her?" He was always to the point; I appreciated that about him, no fucking about.

"Yeah. I think we've just come to an agreement." I raised my eyebrows at Madison, waiting for her acknowledgement. She nodded her head once, which I knew pained her to do. Releasing tension I hadn't realised I was holding, I waited for Scott to continue.

"Good, because Nix just killed Georgie. This shit is really fucked up now."

"Fuck!" I roared. Georgie was Bec's fifteen-year-old

son. Nix and Bec had been together for a year before she recently left him. He'd taken them both out, so his agenda was pretty clear. "You've got Crystal?" That poor kid, Bec's ten-year-old daughter, had lived through some ugly shit and now she was alone in the world.

Madison's eyes were wild; she'd picked up that something bad was going down and snatched the phone out of my hand. "What's happened?"

Tears reformed in her eyes, and broken sobs filled the street as Scott spoke to her. I reached out and touched her on the shoulder; it was an automatic movement and she didn't flinch. It reminded me of a time when things were good between us, but that love didn't exist anymore. We'd killed it.

She ended the call and handed me back my phone before turning around and walking towards the restaurant. I could tell she was wiping the tears from her face.

"What are you doing?" I called out.

Without turning to look at me, she replied, "I'm just saying goodbye to my friends. I'll be right back so wait here."

I let her go. This day had completely turned to shit. And yet, it was fucking good to see Madison.

Shit.

5

─────

MADISON

A s I ENTERED the restaurant to say goodbye, Blake's eyes met mine from across the room. He was mingling with his customers but left them to come to me.

"You okay?" he asked.

I shook my head, tears threatening to spill again, but I pulled my big girl panties up and said, "Not really, but I will be. It turns out that Scott wasn't kidding when he said that there was some bad shit going down. I just found out an old friend of mine was murdered by Nix."

He sucked in a breath. "Fuck, babe. Why?"

I shrugged. "Who knows why Nix does anything he does, but the club thinks it's because she tried to leave him."

His eyes widened in understanding. "So, they think he

will come after you now because you left him. Is that what this is all about?"

"Yes, I think so. Knowing Scott and J though, there's most likely more to it they aren't telling me."

"What are you going to do? Go home?"

"I need some time to think it through, but maybe. My friend's daughter is all alone now so I want to check on her. She's only ten, Blake. How could someone do that to her? Take away her family like that." My chest became heavy as despair travelled through my veins. "I can't believe I dated him. It makes me feel sick."

He pulled me into a hug. "There are some twisted people out there, baby girl. I'm here for you. You know that, right?"

Nodding, I answered, "Yeah, honey. I know I can always count on you."

Stepping out of his embrace, I turned to the table where our friends were. They all watched us intently, probably wondering what the hell was going on. I smiled and left Blake to speak to them.

Serena stood up and came to me with a huge hug. "You've been crying. What the fuck did he say to you?" She was mad on my behalf and I loved that about her.

"I'll fill you in later, okay?" She nodded and I continued, "I'm leaving with J now, so I'll see you when you get home."

"Do you want me to come with you?"

I smiled. "No, I'm okay with him. Besides he looks exhausted and will probably just go to sleep. I need some time alone to think."

"Fair enough, but I won't be home too late."

"Thanks."

I said goodbye to Faith and Rowan, and then headed back outside to J. He sat on his bike waiting for me, still looking as pissed off as he had when he first arrived.

"You ready to go?" he asked.

"Yes, but I'm not so sure I'll be able to get on your bike in this dress."

He smirked. "Never stopped you before, babe," he said, letting his eyes roam over my body. My traitorous body reacted immediately under his gaze, my pulse beating faster and my nipples pebbling.

Flustered, it was easier to be on the defensive. "Just pass me a helmet," I snapped.

He did what I asked and then turned around, settling into his seat while I attempted to hike my dress up enough to allow me to sit behind him. Somehow I managed this; although, I did feel like my ass was exposed for all the world to see.

His hands gripped my legs and pulled me closer to him. Bloody hell, my pussy took immediate notice, and that was not a good thing. Not where J was concerned, because if I let her take control of the situation, God knew where we would end up.

I wrapped my arms around him and held on while we sped off into the night. Fifteen minutes later, we pulled into my driveway. I guessed that Scott had given him my address. Letting go of him, I did my best to get off the bike without flashing too much and quickly smoothed my dress down before removing the helmet and giving it back to him.

Without a second glance in his direction, I went inside

and headed to the kitchen, flipping on lights as I went. I was not one of those people who tried to conserve power or money by never putting lights on; I loved the house lit up. Turning on the tap, I filled the kettle and started making coffee. Figuring J could do with a caffeine hit, I got him a mug too but then stopped myself when I went to fill it. It had been awhile since I'd made him coffee, perhaps he took it differently now.

He entered the kitchen and I turned to him, holding up the coffee and a spoon. "How do you have your coffee these days?"

"Same as before," he replied, leaning against the doorframe and crossing his arms.

I felt a little self-conscious with him watching me like this, but hell would freeze over before I admitted that to him, so I went about the task of making coffee. We stood in silence while waiting for the kettle to boil. It was uncomfortable and I wished that J would say something, *anything*, but he didn't. Eventually, I finished making our drinks and handed his to him before we both took a seat at the kitchen table. And, again, there was complete silence. Normally, I enjoyed silence, but with J it felt awkward.

So I forced myself to say something. "How the hell did Bec end up with Nix?" Both her kids' fathers had been bikers who had screwed her over so the last I knew she'd sworn off bikers altogether.

"From what I can work out she flipped after what happened with Rob and got into some bad shit. Led her to Nix eventually. I think he targeted her."

My mind raced and my anxiety rose. I didn't want to talk about Rob and J had caught me off guard even bringing it up. My hand brushed over the scar on my arm without me realising it, until I saw J's eyes move to it. He lifted his hand and moved to touch me. "Don't," I snapped, and scraped my chair back so I could stand.

"Fuck, Madison. You're still dealing with that, aren't you?" J stood and moved towards me, but I backed away. Reaching his arm out, he hooked it around my waist, and pulled me towards him.

I raised my palms to his chest in an effort to halt his progress of bringing us together. "Don't talk to me about dealing with that. I fucking have. You've got no idea what I've been through with all that shit, so don't think you know all about it." I tried to push away from him but he was too strong and held me close. With my heart beating wildly, I ignored his scent, ignored our closeness. I needed to protect myself. The only way to do that was to keep pushing, and if I couldn't do that physically, my best bet was to stick with the bitch routine.

"You might have dealt with your drinking and I hope you fucking have, babe, but I can tell that you haven't sorted through some of the other shit in your head," he bit out.

"It's none of your business. You made it perfectly clear you weren't interested when you told me to leave," I hissed, and gave him another shove. He relented and let me go.

His face contorted in anger and he raked his fingers through his hair. "Fine. I don't wanna get into this crap right now anyway." He jabbed his finger at me. "Mark my fucking words though, we *will* be getting into it."

Oh, my God. He was still one bossy fucker. And as

much as I tried to ignore the fact, desire screamed through me at his bossiness.

I hope I can be strong enough to stay out of his bed
I pray I can be strong enough to guard my heart.

∾

I ROLLED over and checked the time on the bedside clock. Three a.m. Shit, it was going to be a long night; I'd woken up every hour since I went to bed at midnight. The revelations of the evening had stirred up long suppressed feelings and I couldn't stop the memories. I reached for my smokes and lit one, taking a long, hard drag on it. I closed my eyes as it filled my lungs and the smell of it hit my nostrils. Smoking was a habit I was trying to break, but in times of stress it calmed my nerves. I took another drag, trying desperately to block out the images of Bec suffering at the hands of Nix.

Bec was my best friend growing up. Her father was also a member of the club and we'd been inseparable. She was a few years older than me and had always looked out for me. Bec had fallen pregnant at seventeen, and I had helped her look after Georgie when he was born, and later, Crystal. We'd been through a lot together and had always sworn nothing would come between us, but then on that fateful day that changed my life, something had come between us and there had been no going back from it. Bec cut me out of her life and I'd had to learn how to live life without the unwavering support of a best friend. Even after Nix had fucked me up, she didn't check in on me; she hated me that much. But I had never stopped loving her and my broken heart cracked even more at the realisation that I would never see her again.

Bec's hatred stemmed from the fact she'd been dating Rob at the time he attacked me. They'd been together for a couple of years, and although he'd often flirted with me, I naïvely thought he was harmless. Turned out he was far from harmless. After J killed him, and he and Scott buried the body, Bec had been heartbroken at his disappearance. She wasn't stupid though, and suspected the club had something to do with it because Rob and the club had always had problems. Threats had been made against him so she assumed that the club had finally made good on those threats. And when he'd failed to ever show up again, and I hadn't helped her find him, she turned against me saying that I'd taken the club's side. If only she knew the truth. But I couldn't tell her the truth because it implicated J.

I stubbed out my smoke and left my bed. There was no point trying to force sleep. Wandering out to the kitchen, I saw the light on and realised J was up. He sat at the table and looked up when he heard me. We hadn't spoken much after we'd argued. Before shutting myself away in my bedroom, I'd hooked him up with a pillow and blanket. I didn't trust myself with him yet and needed to work through my conflicting emotions. Although I thought I was over him, especially after the way he'd treated me, relief at seeing him again confused me.

"Scott called. Fucking prospects lost Nix. We're on it, but haven't found him yet," J said as I walked past him to get a glass of water. His voice was husky from sleep and he sat dressed in only his jeans. No freaking shirt. J was easily the best looking man I had ever met and having those muscles shoved in my face at this time of the morning, when I had little sleep was making my brain fire haphazardly. It wasn't safe to be this close to him when he was shirtless. And was that my tattoo still on his chest? Surely not; surely he would have had that removed. I wasn't going to stare to confirm it though.

"You boys are resourceful so I'm sure you'll find him soon." I stumbled over my words distracted by his bare chest and arms.

"Are you taking this seriously, Madison?" he asked sharply.

Annoyed at his tone, all thoughts of his body disappeared. "Of course I am."

"Well, you don't fucking seem like it." He glared at me, waiting for my response.

I decided it was probably best to avoid the rest of this conversation. After finishing my drink, I placed my empty glass in the sink. "I'm going back to bed. I need more sleep to be able to deal with this, J."

His eyes penetrated mine as I walked past him and I wasn't sure what I saw in them. It looked like lust but it was probably anger and frustration. Lack of sleep often led me to the wrong conclusions.

I made my way to my bedroom door and was just closing it when he pushed it open. There was no light on so I could only make him out roughly, but the energy surrounding us was charged.

He stood in the doorway, and as I adjusted to the

darkness, I could tell he was running his eyes over my body. I'd been right when I thought his eyes held lust; he radiated it now. And hell, it turned me on. I'd never wanted any other man like I wanted J. Sure, I loved sex and craved it, but J brought out carnal desires in me that no one else seemed able to.

"J, what are you doing?" I tried hard to concentrate, but found it almost impossible

He took a step toward me and reached out, brushing his thumb across my cheek. "I'd almost gotten to a place where I didn't think about you every fucking day," he murmured, surprising the hell out of me.

His words snapped me out of my lust-fuelled trance and I pushed his hand away from my face. "What the hell?" My body stiffened as I waited for his response. Why was he saying that crap to me? He was the one who told me he didn't love me anymore, the one who sent me away. Why would he still be thinking about me?

"You've no idea, baby. No idea..." he muttered and walked out of the room, leaving me confused and annoyed. J was a walking contradiction, and I sensed this was just the beginning. Events from the past were going to start catching up with me and I was powerless to stop it.

6

JASON

I ROLLED OVER and almost fell out of bed. Shit. It wasn't a bed, it was a couch, and it was the most uncomfortable couch I had ever slept on. Sitting up, I realised what had woken me up. A fucking blender going off in the kitchen. Who the fuck used a blender at this time of the day? Or maybe it was later than I thought. I checked my watch. Nope, it was six o-fucking-clock.

Shifting my legs to put my feet on the ground, I reached for my jeans. I slid into them, threw my t-shirt on, and then stumbled into the kitchen. My guess was that it wasn't Madison. I'd never known her to be a six-a.m.-blender chick. And I was right. I rounded the corner and discovered a chick making a mess with leaves and fruit as she concocted some fucking awful green drink.

As she lifted a glass of it to her lips, I asked, "What the fuck is that?"

She turned, startled, and grumbled, "Morning to you, too. It's a green smoothie."

I rubbed my eyes; it was too early to take all this in. I had never seen anyone drink something that looked that disgusting. "Right," I muttered as I headed to the kettle. "I need coffee."

She pointed at the blender. "There's smoothie left if you want some."

"Not fucking likely," I said, and made coffee as she stood there, sipping her drink and looking me up and down.

"How long you here for?" she eventually asked.

I shrugged. "For as long as it takes."

"For as long as what takes?"

I stopped what I was doing and turned to face her. "For as long as it takes to get Madison to come home with me."

"You do realise that she isn't going to ever go home with you, don't you," she stated matter-of-factly.

I smirked at her. "You don't know Madison as well as you think, sugar."

"My name's Serena, and I know how broken she was when she left Brisbane. She's not going back to that anytime soon."

She scowled at me before starting to clean up her mess. Silence consumed us as we both retreated into our thoughts until a couple of moments later when we were startled by Madison walking into the kitchen. My dick jumped to attention as I took in her sheer t-shirt. It barely covered her ass, and her long legs almost overshadowed her tits. Almost. Because those tits were to fucking die for.

Shit. I concentrated on drinking my coffee. Anything to busy me, and stop me checking her out. However, she made her way to the kettle and when she reached up to grab a mug out of the cupboard, her fucking t-shirt rode up, revealing a perfectly sculpted ass cheek. I let my eyes take that in, and as I looked back up, I saw Serena watching me. Her eyes narrowed and she shot me a filthy look.

Geez, what was up this chick's ass? "You got a problem with me?" I asked, and settled myself back against the counter, crossing one leg over the other, waiting for her answer.

"Yeah, biker boy, I do. I don't like you coming here, after what you did to Maddy years ago, and expecting her to just let you start controlling her. And I don't like your eyes all over her ass. It's not yours anymore."

My eyebrows shot up. I kinda dug this chick, and the way she was loyal to Madison. "Doesn't mean I can't admire it. And as far as me trying to control Madison? Are you sure we're talking about the same Madison? Because the one I used to fuck never let me control her."

Madison dropped her mug and it smashed across the floor. I flicked my gaze to her and found her eyes narrowed at me and her lips pressed together in the way she used to when I'd pissed her off.

"Classy, J. Fucking classy." She dropped to the floor to start cleaning up the mess. This made my day, and I continued to check out her ass and legs while she did it. Serena helped her, but not before pinning me with another glower

Perfect. I'd succeeded in pissing them both off. Time

to get out of there for a while. "Towels in the bathroom?" I asked, pushing off the counter.

"Yes, in the cupboard," Madison replied, her voice sharp.

I took one last look at her ass and then made my way to the bathroom for a shower, making sure to throw Serena a wink on my way out.

MADISON

SERENA and I watched J leave. "What an asshole!" She didn't hold back.

I laughed at her indignation. "He's worked out how to push your buttons, honey. That's all."

She gaped at me. "Are you standing up for him?"

"Not really, but he's not always like that. I have my issues with him, and yes I do think he was an asshole to me years ago, but what he said to you just then... that was J messing with you."

Her forehead wrinkled. "Yeah, well, I'm withholding judgement for now. I still call asshole."

We finished cleaning up the mess I'd made and then I helped her finish cleaning up her smoothie mess. "I don't know how you can drink these things," I said.

"That's exactly what biker boy said."

"Yeah, I doubt J even knew what it was."

"So, now he's here, are we still going shopping today

or are you pulling out? Plus, I still need you to fill me in on what he told you last night," she said.

I considered her question for a moment. "I don't see why we can't still go shopping." Why should we let J interfere with our plans?

She raised her brows. "You really think he's going to let you out of his sight?"

"Well, if he doesn't, it just means he's coming shopping too. I highly doubt he'll want to do that."

"Ha! Good luck with that, *sugar*," she said. "I'm going to go and get ready just in case we're allowed out." Her eyes danced with sarcasm and I laughed as she turned and left me. Once someone had rubbed Serena the wrong way like J had, it took a lot of work on their behalf to win her over. I had no idea if J planned to try, but he had a long road ahead of him if he did.

I made the coffee I'd originally come to make and sat at the table, enjoying the quiet while I drank it. My thoughts wandered to my conversation with J the previous night. His admission confused me, and although I wanted to know what he meant, there was no way I'd ever bring it up with him. My heart was still fragile where he was concerned. Before I left Brisbane, we'd been rebuilding our friendship and I'd been sure we'd end up back together again, after I managed to free myself of Nix. But then Nix turned on me, and J had been the one to find me beaten and bloody. Something snapped in him that day, and our friendship changed again. A week later, he came to me and told me there was nothing left between us and that I should leave Brisbane to get away from Nix, to start a new life. He'd sent me away; he didn't love or want me anymore.

Startling me from my thoughts, J came back into the kitchen, freshly showered. I took in his jeans and the way his fitted black t-shirt defined his muscles. And then his scent filled the room: sandalwood. God, I loved that smell; it was the one he'd always worn. It hit my nostrils and then it hit my heart. Memories flooded my mind and overwhelmed my senses. It was funny how a smell had the power to bring so much back to you.

Ignoring the weak sensation in my legs, I stood and, at the same time, he moved into my space. *Too close.* His presence, his smell, his breath – it all messed with me and I couldn't think straight. Our eyes locked for a few silent seconds, and then I stepped backwards to escape whatever was happening between us.

"I'm sorry for being an asshole to your friend before," he apologised, shocking the shit out of me.

This was a new side to J. I tilted my head to the side. "Since when do you apologise for things you've said?"

He shrugged. "Since now. Since I'm trying to get you to stop being angry at me. I know you're still mad at me for what I did, but, babe, that was two years ago and we need to move forward if you're gonna come back home. Be a lot easier to do that if you weren't so hostile."

"Who said I was coming back to Brisbane?"

"You'll be coming back with me. That's a given. Just a matter of time till you agree."

"You're still as cocky and bossy as you always were, aren't you?"

Before he could reply, Serena waltzed back in and said to J, "So, biker boy, Madison and I have shopping planned for today. Will you be coming with us or will you allow us to go out on our own?"

J smirked, and then looking from Serena to me, he said, "I like your friend, even if she does have a smart mouth on her." Focusing his gaze on Serena, he replied in a firm voice, "And, no, there won't be any shopping today."

Her body straightened and she held his gaze. "Maybe not for you. We'll be going though."

He stepped closer to her, all lightness gone from his eyes. Nobody said no to J. "No, you won't be, sweetheart."

Her eyes widened. Serena wasn't used to men like J, men who said no to her. And she certainly wasn't used to being spoken to in a forceful tone like the one J had just used. She quickly looked to me for backup.

"J, I think we'll be okay shopping. I highly doubt Nix will be out looking for us in a shopping mall." I tried to reason with him.

He turned his head in my direction. *Oh, shit.* The look flashing in his eyes was not one I wanted to mess with. "Did you not fucking take in what I told you about Nix last night? Do you need to see those photos again or perhaps I should show them to Serena so she can fully appreciate what we're dealing with here," he fumed, reaching for his phone.

I held up my hand. "Stop! No, we don't need to see those photos. We won't go shopping." I gave in, but I wasn't happy that Nix had yet again managed to disrupt our lives.

He opened his mouth to speak but changed his mind

before stalking out of the room without uttering another word.

"What the fuck, Madison?" Serena rounded on me.

I held up both my palms to silence her. "Not now, honey." I paused for a moment to think, but nothing came. "Fuck it, I need a smoke!" I left in search of one.

Five minutes later, I was outside, smoke in one hand, phone in the other. I needed Blake.

He answered on the first ring. "How's it going over there, baby girl?"

"Well, J's telling us what we can and can't do. Serena's mad at both of us, and I'm hiding outside having a smoke. What does that tell you?"

"Do you want me to come over?"

This was what made Blake a superstar in my eyes. Even with his busy schedule at the restaurant, he was willing to drop everything for me. "No, don't do that. I just needed to hear your voice; it always makes me feel better."

"Have you decided what you're going to do?"

I sighed, and blew out a long breath of cigarette smoke. "I don't want to go back, but I probably will just so I can make sure Crystal, my friend's daughter, is okay."

"Yeah, I get that. I would do the same thing."

A loud bang sounded from inside the house. "Shit, Blake, I've got to go. I'll call you later, okay?" I said, putting my smoke out.

"Yeah, babe. Later," he said, and hung up.

Heading inside, I yelled out, "What happened?"

I found them both in the laundry. Turned out the noise I'd heard was the dryer falling off the wall. "Bloody hell, how did that happen?" I asked.

Serena's cheeks reddened. "I may have slammed the dryer door really hard and, as a result, the dryer may have fallen down."

J stood with his back to me as he inspected the wall. God, I hoped he could fix this because our landlord would not be happy. He looked around at me. "I can fix this. But it'll mean a trip for all of us to the hardware store."

Serena rolled her eyes. "How did I know you were gonna say that," she grumbled.

"Sure, just let me get dressed," I said, and left them to bicker while I went to find some clothes.

Something told me we were in for one long ass day.

7

MADISON

THE TRIP to the hardware store was a torturous experience. Serena constantly took shots at J, who in turn, argued back. By the end of it, I was ready to stab myself in the eyes and cut my ears off; anything not to have to see or hear either of them.

I was thankful, however, that J managed to pick up all the supplies he would need to fix the mess in our laundry. He and I argued over the bill. In the end, he won and paid the bill. Men!

At home, J was busy being Mr. Handyman, while Serena and I were lounging in front of the television. I'd just filled her in on everything J had told me last night.

"Shit, what are you going to do?" she asked.

"I don't know." I sighed.

"Okay, so you want to check on Crystal. Yes?" Serena loved helping me solve my dramas.

I nodded. "Yes."

"So, you go home for a visit. You check on your girl, you hang out with your family for a bit, you stay until they sort this Nix mess out. Then you come back here and live happily ever after." She smiled, happy with her own advice.

I groaned out of frustration. "You make it sound so easy when it is as far from easy as anything could be. This shit with Nix could take a long time. I might kill my family if I have to stay that long. And what am I going to do about J?"

"Yeah, biker boy poses a problem," she mused.

"I love how, after everything I just said, all you heard was the bit about J."

"Oh no, honey, I heard it all. But the only problem in all of that was him."

I raised my eyebrows. "Why?"

She smiled her wicked little smile. "I'd say that's pretty obvious. You're both still hot for each other so I'm worried about where that would lead."

I buried my face in my hands. "Shit, I'm screwed, aren't I?" I said, and then looking up, I continued, "I don't understand my feelings. He broke my heart and yet, here I am, wanting him all over again. What is wrong with me?"

"You could just fuck him and get that out of your system," she suggested.

I considered it for a moment. She was right. I could totally fuck J. It was what I did these days anyway – fuck and run. But would I... could I walk away, and be happy with just sex? Fuck it, this was the new me, the stronger me. The me who didn't let a guy stomp on my heart anymore. Of course, I could do it. I smiled at Serena. "Thanks, babe. I might just do that."

J FINISHED up in the laundry a few hours later. I was impressed with his work, as was Serena. She even appeared to warm to him a little, offering him a drink when he was finished.

"Thanks," he said, when she made her offer, "And the next time you want to take your anger out on something, I'd suggest you choose a different target."

She glared at him before leaving to get his drink. I rolled my eyes. "You like pissing her off, don't you?" I said.

He chuckled, eyes twinkling. "She's too easy to play with, babe."

Before we could continue this conversation, his phone rang and he went outside to take the call. I traipsed into the kitchen in search of Serena.

"I might just throw this at him instead of giving it to him," she muttered.

I laughed. "You do know he's just playing with you, don't you?"

"Yeah, well, I don't want to play with him. He rubs me the wrong way."

"Fair enough, honey. Do you want me to take him his drink?"

"Yes!" she exclaimed, shoving it at me.

I took it from her and headed outside. J was still on

his call when I got to him. He looked up and caught my gaze. There was no smile, but there was certainly some heat there. I watched as his eyes moved, slowly, hungrily, over my body while he continued his conversation. By the time his eyes found mine again, every nerve ending of mine had stirred with desire and my fingers ached to touch him. Butterflies danced in my stomach and my core clenched in anticipation. I wanted him. He ended his call, put his phone in his pocket, and walked to where I stood.

"That mine?" he asked, nodding at the glass.

"Yes." I forced the word out as I handed him the drink. Bewildered from the way he'd undressed me with his eyes, I was having trouble thinking straight, let alone forming words.

He drank some water, but kept his eyes on mine the whole time. I didn't know where this was heading, but I was beginning to feel completely exposed to him, like he was reading my thoughts, and desires.

Needing to put some space between us, I moved to leave but he reached out and grabbed my wrist. "You feel it too, don't you?" he said, his voice low and hoarse.

I avoided his eyes and, instead, focused on his hand holding my wrist. He let me go and put his finger under my chin, tilting my head up to look at him. I wanted to squeeze my eyes shut; I didn't want to look at him, and I really didn't want to look inside myself for the answer to his question.

Instead, I jerked my hand out of his hold, and said, "It doesn't mean anything, J."

"You sure about that, babe?"

Determined not to hide away, I looked directly into his eyes. "Yes, I'm very sure," I replied, even though I was pretty damn sure I was lying.

He contemplated me for a couple of moments, and then slowly nodded, like he'd settled something in his mind. Then he changed the subject. "Still no word on Nix's whereabouts."

"So we're still on lockdown?"

"Yeah."

"Okay. I'm pretty tired after not much sleep last night, so I'm going to have a nap," I said. I also needed some time to myself; these unwanted desires and confused thoughts needed to go into lockdown too as far as I was concerned.

I left him outside and told my pussy to shut the hell up. She wasn't getting any today.

～

I SLEPT ALL AFTERNOON, waking around dinner time. J and Serena had managed to not kill each other. In fact, they were in the kitchen, cooking dinner together when I found them.

I sat at the table and asked, "Have you two been playing nice?"

Serena poked her tongue out at me. "As a matter of fact, we have been. J changed the oil in my car and checked some other things too."

My eyebrows shot up. "Really? How did she convince you to do that?"

He smirked. "Let's just say she had her ways."

Serena flicked him with the tea towel, almost playfully. "You make it sound dirty, biker boy," she said, and then directed at me, "I cooked cupcakes for him."

I had to stop myself from laughing at that. "Where's the mess from your cooking, honey?" I asked, surveying the almost-spotless kitchen. I was always the one who had to clean up her kitchen messes so I wondered who the heck had done this one.

"J cleaned it up," Serena replied, and I didn't fail to notice that she seemed kind of impressed about this.

J was a clever man; winning my friend over by doing things for her. I looked at him and found him watching me, smile in place. Yeah, he knew what he was doing all right. The only question was – *why was he going to the effort?*

∼

THE REST of the weekend passed pretty uneventfully. J continued reporting that Nix hadn't been found yet, so we stayed home all weekend, only heading out for food and movies. After a short-lived truce, Serena and J returned to their bickering. Because I knew J, I could tell he enjoyed it, and when I tried to point this out to Serena, she rolled her eyes and complained that he should go home. Having no experience of the world I'd grown up in, I didn't think she realised just how dangerous Nix was. I shuddered to think what he would do if he found us, but I didn't share this with her. J didn't push the point either. In fact, he seemed to be going out of his way to keep things light;

perhaps that was why he insisted on playing with Serena –
to keep the focus off the reason why we were stuck
at home.

Monday morning rolled around, and Serena and I had
to go to work. J tried to talk me out of going, but I stood
my ground, so at nine o'clock the three of us arrived at the
boutique. I tried to convince him we'd be all right without
a minder, but he refused to listen.

Gina, our boss, greeted us with a smirk. Eyeing J as he
stood outside the shop, she said, "I heard you had a
bodyguard but they never told me he was this hot." Gina
was Blake's sister; he must have told her about J. She was
a kickass boss and I loved her hard. Unfortunately, she had
no filter and said whatever came to her in the moment.

"Yeah, sorry, he'll be hanging out here today," I
apologised.

"No need to say sorry, darl. Frankly, you've made my
day. I do love me some eye candy," she said with a wink.

We got to work, restocking the shelves and cleaning
while J stayed outside for most of the morning. He seemed
busy on his phone and I was grateful I didn't have to deal
with him in the shop.

Being around him was hard; old feelings kept
resurfacing and I alternated between hurt, anger and lust.
Every now and then, I caught glimpses of the J I had
loved, and those times were the hardest. They hit me fair
in the chest. I wondered if he had a girlfriend currently. We
hadn't really even had a friendly conversation about our
lives since he'd been here so I had no clue what he'd been
up to over the last couple of years. Jealousy wrapped itself

around my heart when I thought of him being with someone else.

I don't want to know.

Fuck.

Who was I kidding? I had a desperate need to know these details of his life.

I mentally slapped myself. It was time to get my shit together.

"So, darl, have you decided if you're going to head up to Brisbane?" Gina approached me.

I sighed. I hated this question. "I think I'm going to have to, even though I don't want to. But I don't want to leave you stuck for staff."

She waved her hand. "Don't worry about me or the shop. We'll sort something out. I just want to make sure you're safe. And I want you to go tomorrow."

My eyes widened. "Are you sure?"

"Yes, absolutely. You stay away as long as you need, and your job will be here when you come back," she promised.

I gave her a huge hug. "Has anyone ever told you that you're the best boss?"

"Oh, they don't need to. I already know I am," she replied, her eyes dancing with naughtiness. "Now, you go and have your lunch break and then Serena can have hers."

I grabbed my purse and headed outside. J was on the phone, but saw me come outside and signalled for me to wait.

"I'm going to buy lunch, J. And I only get an hour so I don't have a lot of time because the place where I buy lunch is always busy," I said. He kept talking so I turned and walked towards the cafe where I always bought lunch. He could catch up.

I could hear him muttering something into the phone and then silence for a moment before he barked, "Madison!"

The last thing I wanted to do was stop for him, but there was something in his tone, a don't-fuck-with-me command. So I halted my progress and turned back to him.

He stalked to where I waited. "Why the fuck do you have to be so difficult about this?" The vein in his neck pulsed and his hands clenched by his sides.

I stared at him, unsure where his harsh words came from. "About what? Waiting for you so I can buy lunch?"

Be expelled a long breath and raked his fingers through his hair. "No, about everything. I thought we were on the same page, but then you insist on working today and then you don't wait for me to walk you to lunch. I'm just trying to keep you safe and you're doing everything to make that hard."

"Maybe it has something to do with the way Scott has gone about this. And the fact that he sent you." I knew I was being irrational, but all my old hurt had resurfaced. Hurt that I'd never fully dealt with. Unfortunately it manifested itself as anger.

He flinched. It was only for a second, and most people wouldn't have even noticed it. But I knew J, and I saw it. It surprised the hell out of me. "Well then, it looks like we've got some shit to sort out, babe, because I'm not going anywhere."

"I don't want to sort shit out with you. That ship sailed two fucking years ago, J," I spat.

He gripped my arm, pulling me closer. "No, it fucking didn't," he growled, eyes blazing, "And you can't deny there's still something here. I feel it and I know you feel it too."

I laughed. No, actually, I cackled. "You wanna fuck, J? I can feel *that*, and yeah, if you wanna go there, I'm all for it. But don't mistake my desire for your cock for anything else."

He let me go, and looked at me with disgust. "When the fuck did you get so bitchy?"

I settled icy eyes on his. "The day you ripped my fucking heart out, asshole." We glared at each other for a few moments and then I said, "Now, can we go and get lunch?"

"Lead the way, sweetheart," he grit out, and I didn't miss the way he said 'sweetheart', like I was the furthest thing from his sweetheart.

My heart cracked a little more, even though I didn't think it was possible. And fuck him for that.

8

MADISON

I UNZIPPED MY bag and then answered my ringing phone, balancing it between my shoulder and ear so I could continue packing my clothes. It was Tuesday morning, and after talking it over with Serena and getting her opinion on the situation, I knew it was time to leave. J seemed immeasurably happy about this, as did Scott. I was yet to talk with my father about this, which surprised me. I figured he would have called by now. He usually had something to say about everything I did, or at least that was how it felt to me. Since moving to Coffs Harbour, I'd managed to lessen his involvement in my life and even my mother had stepped back and given me the space to live as I wished. She was the kind of woman who had to have a say in just about everything involving her family. The thought of returning to the club had caused me some sleepless nights. I'd fought hard for my independence and wasn't about to give that up for anybody.

"Hello?" I answered the phone.

"Madison," — it was Blake — "what time are you leaving?"

"Soon, honey. Have you got time to come over so I can say goodbye?" I really needed to see him before I left.

"I'll be there," he replied and we hung up.

I opened my closet and started throwing clothes into my bag.

Serena breezed in and sat on my bed watching me pack. "That man of yours is moody. I've been trying to make conversation but I give up," she said.

"Let's get something straight. He isn't my man," I said, as I finished packing.

"Why did you two break up?" she asked.

I sighed and sat down on the bed next to her. "There were a lot of reasons we broke up, but he was the one who ended it when I accused him of cheating on me. When I found out later that he didn't cheat, I thought we might have had a chance at getting back together but stuff happened, and he told me to get out of the club, to leave town. He was done with me."

"Fucker." She rocked a dirty look – best friends were the shit. I loved that Serena never pressured me for more information than I was willing to give. Even though we'd been best friends for two years now, she'd never pushed me to talk about this stuff from my past. She knew I had been through something that I didn't like to talk about, and knew that I had a messy breakup, but was happy enough to leave it at that.

"Yeah, fucker." I grinned and hugged her. "God, I'm going to miss you."

She hugged me hard and then pulled away. "I know. Me too. Maybe I could come and visit soon," she said.

I shook my head. "I don't think you should, honey. From what J and Scott have told me, it's pretty messed up at the moment. I don't want you getting mixed up in all of that."

"Fuck that. I can't leave my best girl alone when she needs me. I'm sure that J and his boys can look out for both of us."

I laughed. "You've got no clue but I do love you. Now, get your ass off the bed and help me carry my stuff out of here."

As we entered the living room, we ran into Blake who'd just walked through the front door. He pulled me into a hug and we stayed like that for a few moments. It would be tough leaving him as I'd come to depend upon him over the last two years. He was my voice of reason when my level of crazy hit epic proportions, and he was the steady influence in my life.

"You know where I am if you need me, baby girl," he murmured in my ear and then let me go.

My eyes met his and I smiled at him, "Absolutely. You'd better keep your phone close all the time because I'm sure I'll be calling you often. I'll need you to talk some sense into me when I lose my shit. Okay?"

He nodded and grabbed my hand and squeezed it. "I mean it, Maddy, if you need me, I'm there."

A phone started ringing and I looked around to catch J staring intently at Blake and me. He stood in the doorway between the kitchen and living room, and I hadn't heard him come in. It was his phone ringing but he wasn't rushing to answer it.

"Are you going to get that?" I asked with a brow raise.

He stared at me for another moment before finally silencing the phone. "What?" he barked into it and walked back into the kitchen, away from us.

I turned back to Blake and Serena. "Are Rowan and Faith able to come and say goodbye?"

"No, they're busy, but I think they'll both give you a call later on," Blake answered. He jerked his head towards J and asked, "What was that all about?"

I shrugged. "I have no idea." And I really didn't. J could be a moody bastard and I figured he was just in one of his moods, especially because of what was happening with Nix and the club.

"Are you sure you want him to take you back home? I could drive you," he offered.

"No, I'll go with J," I said quickly and Blake raised his eyebrows at me.

Shit. That was pretty eager of me. Fuck, this wasn't good. I needed to keep my distance from J.

"No, maybe you could drive me." I changed my mind and looked to Blake who was nodding in agreement.

"Madison is with me," J growled, and I turned around to find him almost right behind me. He caught me by surprise and as I stumbled back a little, his hand shot out to catch me from falling. His arm snaked around my waist and he held me firmly. I looked up at him as he stepped closer to me; our breath mingled and my stomach clenched with that feeling of anticipation that I hadn't known since we broke up. "You'll ride with me. It's safer," he ordered.

"I think Madison can make her own mind up," Blake retorted.

J tore his eyes from mine to glare at Blake. "Did you not fucking hear me the first time? She rides with me."

"You're joking, aren't you?" Blake snorted. "Madison is a grown woman and can make her own decisions."

"Do I look like I'm fucking joking?" J challenged, and I realised it was time to cut in before this got out of hand. Blake was still being polite, probably for my sake, but if push came to shove, he wouldn't hesitate to take J on.

I laid a hand on J's chest and said to Blake, "It's okay, I'll ride with J. He's right. With Nix off their radar it'll be safer for me to stick with him."

Blake and J continued glaring at each other, and I pushed on J's chest and pulled myself out of his hold. "Are we going?" I asked him impatiently.

He looked away from Blake to me and nodded. "Yeah, I'll get our stuff and meet you outside." With that, he gathered up our belongings and headed out to his bike, shooting Blake one last glare before he left.

"Like I said, moody," Serena stated and looped her arm through mine as we followed him out. She turned her head to me with a wicked glint, "I bet he's fucking intense in bed, right?"

"Oh, my God! We are not going there." I shook my head in exasperation. Serena had a one track mind most days.

She laughed and I couldn't help but join her; she really was the sunshine in my life.

I GRABBED Blake and Serena in a group hug. "I'll call you once we're there. Should be in about four or five hours."

J was waiting for me on his bike. Sensing his impatience, I finished my goodbyes and climbed on behind him. Apart from the other night, it had been years since I'd been on the back of a bike and it felt good. I'd missed it. Wrapping my arms around his waist, I tried to wipe away the thoughts of just how good it felt to be on *his* bike. He pulled my hands together so I was holding him tighter and pleasure shot through my body at his touch. I wondered if he felt it too, but quickly dismissed that thought; after all, he was the one who hadn't wanted to pursue a relationship again two years ago. I doubted he'd changed his mind.

We took off and I settled in for a long trip. It would give me some time to sort through my feelings about going home. And about J. After I moved, I'd never heard from him, and hadn't intended to see him again. I didn't want to want him again, but the heart can't be led. I was trusting and hoping like hell that my heart knew J had the power to break me again.

9

JASON

I LEANED INTO the doorframe of the clubhouse bar, crossed my arms in front of me and settled back to watch the duel between Scott and Madison. We'd been back barely fifteen minutes and they were already at it.

"I don't want you going to see Crystal now because I can't go with you. I've gotta be somewhere else." Scott's body tensed as he argued with her. He and Madison had a long history of battles, both as stubborn as the other.

"I can take a prospect with me," she suggested.

My eyes wandered down to her hips where she had placed her hands. She wore the tightest fucking jeans, and I figured all the assholes in the room were probably mentally undressing her. I wanted to tell them to all fuck off, but I had no right to those thoughts anymore.

Scott was pacing. Jesus Christ, if he was like this with

his sister, what the fuck would he be like with an old lady? He didn't do relationships and that was probably a good thing because his over protectiveness wouldn't be appreciated by many women. I should fucking know. I had those tendencies too, and it had caused no end of problems between Madison and I when we were together.

"Fuck it," Scott swore, and tipped his chin in my direction. "J will go with you then."

I pushed off from my leaning spot and walked towards them. Madison swung around to face me, a frown on her face.

"J doesn't have to go with me." She looked wildly around the room until her gaze stopped on Stoney who sat in the corner. She jabbed a finger towards him. "Stoney can go with me."

"I will go with you, Madison," I growled. "Get your stuff and we can leave now."

"Madison." We all stopped and turned at the voice of our president. Marcus Cole was a commanding presence and I watched Madison shrink a little. She'd always had a difficult relationship with her father. He was a man used to being in control and unfortunately for him, had raised a daughter who was too much like him, so they were constantly arguing.

She composed herself. "Dad."

"Go with J for fuck's sake. Not sure why you have to always fucking argue with everything." He could be a bastard sometimes and I squeezed my fists, itching to punch him for being so harsh to her.

"Nice to see you too," she seethed.

Marcus ignored her and turned to me. "Take her to

see Crystal and then bring her back here. I want her staying at the clubhouse until we find Nix." With that, he strode out of the room without a backwards glance at Madison. Hurt crossed her face, and I fought the urge to pull her close and wrap my arms around her. Instead, I silently stayed where I was, waiting for her to make the next move.

"Nothing much changes around here, does it?" she asked no one in particular and threw her hands in the air. "Fuck! Is it any wonder I didn't want to come home?" She directed this one at me.

Shit, I didn't want to get into family fucking politics. It had been a long day and it wasn't over yet. I pointed at the front door. "Time to go," I said, walking towards it and then looked back over my shoulder at Scott. "I'll check in with you later, see where we're at."

He nodded. "Yeah. Later, brother."

MADISON

WELL, my father hadn't changed much since I last saw him, still as controlling as ever. He and Scott were the same. How the hell was I going to get through this visit? And J, well, that was a whole other headache. The mixed signals he threw out gave me whiplash. One minute he acted as if being around me was a hardship and the next he looked at me like he used to.

I followed him outside and walked to his bike while he

stopped and spoke with a guy I had never seen before. They discussed something in hushed tones and I could tell from J's facial expressions that he wasn't happy with whatever had been said. He muttered something at the guy before shaking his head at him in disgust. This couldn't be good.

"What was that all about?" I asked as he approached me.

"Nothing you need to worry about," he dismissed me.

My blood boiled. "Why do you, Scott and Dad do that? Why can't you just answer my questions rather than always dismissing them?"

J turned his angry eyes to me. "Not everything is about you, Madison. Seems to be something you still haven't figured out."

I flinched at his words and swallowed back my hurt. His anger felt undeserved. I'd changed a lot in the last two years but he seemed set on believing I was still the same person. Taking a deep breath, I attempted to explain where I was coming from. "Yes, I know that, but with what's happening, I figured it might be about Nix. And *that* is about me."

"Yeah, baby, *that* is about you," he snapped back at me. "But this isn't. Now get on the back of the bike and let's go."

Oh, no he didn't. "What does that mean, J? The bit about that being about me." There had been an ugly tone to his words that I didn't like and I struggled to understand their origin.

He leant down into my face and the anger emanating

from him stunned me. "Perhaps all of this shit wouldn't be happening if you hadn't dated Nix."

Tears threatened my eyes. "I can't believe you just said that," I whispered, staring at him in shock and confusion. He stayed bent and in my face, glaring at me while the hurt feelings and unsaid things from years ago sat painfully in the space between us.

Finally, he stood back and broke eye contact. "Crystal's staying with Brooke, so be prepared for that." He changed the subject just like that; just like he always used to do and it hurt just as much now as it had then.

BROOKE WAS J'S SISTER, and we had a long, hard history. Back in school we were close, but the year after we finished school, a misunderstanding had come between us. It was a silly misunderstanding, about a guy, and she'd hated me ever since. Bec, however, had remained friends with Brooke, so she'd continued to be a presence in my life. However, we did our best to keep out of each other's way. When I started dating J, she'd been pissed off and had done her best to break us up. Brooke was the only family J had left after both their parents had died in a car accident and he was very close to her. She was his younger sister and he looked out for her and made sure she was always okay. When she began her campaign against us, it had almost worked because J always made excuses for her behaviour. I'd often felt like I came second to her and had threatened to walk away from the relationship a couple of times. It all came to a head about a year into our relationship and J had been forced to take a stance. He chose me, but it was always clear how much he loved Brooke, and from then on, I tried hard not to put him in the middle again. I think Brooke did the same because she stopped trying to separate us.

We pulled up at Brooke's house about fifteen minutes later. J was still shitty, and stalked into the house ahead of me. I watched as he entered the building and greeted Brooke. She looked past him at me, her face a blank mask. I was surprised when she gave me a tight smile and gestured for me to come in.

"Madison, how are you?" she asked as I came through the front door.

Well, shit, I could make small talk too. "I'm okay. And you?"

Before she could answer, Crystal came running into the room. "Madison!" She threw herself into my arms and I was overcome with emotion. I bent down and wrapped her in my arms, smoothing her hair and pressing my lips to her forehead. My heart broke a little more for her and I fought back the tears. I struggled with the knowledge that this beautiful child was now alone in the world, and I was annoyed at myself for not coming to see her sooner.

"Hey, sweetheart," I said, holding her a moment longer, and then I pulled away to take in her eyes. They betrayed her confusion, her loss and her heartbreak. If I was upset before, I was murderous now. How dare Nix take away her family? I kissed her again and then stood, keeping my arm around her.

J was watching me intently; his pissed off mood

somewhat abated. He knelt in front of Crystal. "How would you like us to stay for dinner tonight, angel?" he asked as he ran his hand over her hair in a soothing gesture. "We could order in your favourite."

He was gentle with her and my heart skipped a beat. It reminded me there was a softer side to J – in there somewhere, under all that rough biker bullshit.

Crystal nodded at him. "My favourite is pizza," she said, her voice timid.

J smiled at her and said, "Okay, I'll order that. You go and sit with Madison while Brooke and I organise dinner." His tenderness was killing me. He was so hot and cold; one minute so angry with me that he was saying shit I didn't know he had in him, and then this, this sweet talk to a child.

He stood and motioned for Brooke to follow him into the kitchen, leaving Crystal and I alone to talk. I hadn't seen her in over three years, but before that we had been almost as close as a mother and daughter. Bec had been raising her kids on her own and I was her support, helping her out with money, babysitting and anything else she needed. Coming back into Crystal's life now, after three years, I had been worried she might not remember me but I was relieved that she did.

I took her hand and led her to the couch. "Sweetheart, I'm so sorry I haven't been here for you. Not only now but also for the last few years. Things happened, and your Mum and I—"

She cut me off. "Mum told me that she never wanted to see you again. I know it wasn't you who didn't want to see me." Her voice broke up as she got her last few words out and her shoulders drooped. Tears began pooling in her sad, green eyes and my chest ached at her grief.

I nodded. "I need you to know that I am here for you now, baby. I won't leave you alone. Do you understand that?"

She started crying and I used every ounce of control to stay strong for her. The last thing she needed was me crying with her; instead, she needed to know I was strong enough for the both of us, that I would get her through this. I pulled her to me and hugged her, letting her cry. Crystal had always been a tough little girl, fiercely independent and I hadn't seen her cry much over the years. She tended to bottle her feelings up and tried not to let us see what she was going through. I was sure it was her way of coping with all the crazy shit she had witnessed in her life. Bec had been as good a mother as she could be, but the men she had been involved with had often brought the crazy to her life and, as a result, the kids felt it too. Having grown up in the club lifestyle myself, I could always see why Crystal shut herself off like that because I had done the same as a child.

We sat there quietly and I held her close while she sobbed. I wondered if this was the first time she had let herself feel her grief. A week earlier, she had her family. Now she had no one. No one but me and a club of bikers who would, I guessed, do anything to protect her. In that moment, I knew I would make damn sure they protected her. Even if it meant moving back here; the place I had sworn never to return to.

~

DINNER WAS STRAINED BUT BROOKE, J and I did our best to keep it friendly for Crystal's sake. After dinner, we moved back to the living room and watched some television. Crystal was subdued and fairly exhausted so Brooke suggested she have a shower and go to bed early. She agreed and headed off to the bathroom while Brooke went to clean up the kitchen. This left J and I alone, and we sat in silence watching the television. I had no idea what we were watching because my mind was racing with so many questions; not only about Crystal but also about him and me. I hadn't been able to stop thinking about his angry outburst earlier.

I looked over at him and found him watching me. He didn't break eye contact, just continued to watch me. My stomach tensed as unease washed over me; I didn't know what he was thinking anymore. When we were together, I used to be able to read him most of the time, but over two years later, I had no idea of the thoughts running through his mind. Hell, maybe I never knew him as well as I thought I did. He had, after all, told me to leave right when I thought we had a chance to be together again.

I finally broke the silence. "Have you guys found Nix yet?" I went with an easy question.

"No, but Scott's got a lead so he's chasing that up tonight," he answered, eyes still firmly on mine.

"What's the plan for Crystal? Do you think she's safe here?"

He dragged his hand through his hair and sighed. "We've got two guys watching the house. We're doing what we can to keep her safe."

"How long will she stay here with Brooke?"

"She'll be living with Brooke now. It was what Bec wanted," he said quietly, as he watched for my reaction. He would have known what was to come.

I shot out of the chair. "What the fuck, J? Why would she do that?"

He reacted sharply, standing and grabbing my arm. "Keep your voice down, Madison," he snapped. "Bec and Brooke were close after you left. It's definitely what she wanted."

I yanked my arm out of his grip. "Well, I'm going to be around to help so Brooke will just have to deal with that."

His eyes widened. "You're staying? For good?"

I nodded. "Yes." I'd been grappling with the decision, but as soon as the words left my mouth, I knew it was the right one. A sense of peace settled within me.

Tension thickened in the air as J silently watched me.

He doesn't want me to stay.

That hurt.

Deep.

And it shouldn't have.

God, why am I even allowing what he thinks to upset me? I've moved on. I don't care what he thinks anymore.

I pushed my shoulders back and took a deep breath. "Yes, J, like it or not, I'm staying so you'd better get used to it." Without waiting for his response, I walked outside, in desperate need of a moment to myself to clear my head.

∼

TEN MINUTES LATER, I was considerably calmer after giving myself a pep talk. J was smart enough to give me that space. I'd taken a step towards the house to head back inside when he came out.

"You've missed a call," he said, handing me my phone before going back inside.

I checked to see who had called and smiled when I saw it was Serena. Shit, I was supposed to call her when we arrived. I called her back and waited for her to answer.

"Bitch, I was worried!" she chastised me.

"Honey, calm down. I'm sorry I didn't call. I got side-tracked by Scott and Dad, who are being their usual bossy selves. And, don't get me started on J."

"Oh, please do get started on J," she quipped.

I laughed and just like that, she broke through my anger and hurt and reminded me how much I needed her in my life. "He's making me crazy!"

"Mmmm, what's he doing? Besides getting your girl bits in a tizz?"

"He said that if I hadn't dated Nix, none of this would be happening." I answered her, the words tearing at my heart.

"Wow. Holy shit. He might be a hot guy but what an asshole. I hope you told him where to go."

"He caught me off guard. I never expected him to say something like that to me. He's confusing the hell out of me. I just don't know what to make of it."

"Just keep him at a distance, okay. Do what you went there to do, and then you can come home and forget all about him again."

I paused for a moment and then sighed. "I wish I

could, honey, but I've made a decision. I'm going to move back here to be close to Crystal and look out for her."

"I thought you might decide to do that. You're a good woman, Madison Cole, and don't let anyone tell you otherwise, especially not J," she said, and I loved her a little more for her unconditional support.

"I'm going to miss you. Maybe you should move here too," I said, meaning every word.

"Never say never, huh. Gonna visit you real soon, though," she replied, "And I'll kick J's ass if he's being a fucker to you."

I had no doubt about that. "Okay, I'd better go. Can you tell Blake I'll call him tomorrow? I love you, honey."

"Will do. Love you, too, girl," she said and hung up.

I went back inside, hoping to say goodbye to Crystal and convince J to take me back to the clubhouse. I didn't want to hang around Brooke's for much longer.

Brooke and Crystal were back in the living room with J, and they were all laughing at something on the television. J looked over at me and then tapped Crystal on the shoulder. "Say goodnight to Madison, angel. We have to go in a minute," he said, and I was relieved he had the same plans as I did.

Crystal gave me a long hug and I whispered in her ear, "I love you, baby girl, and I'll be back to see you soon."

She kissed me and then left with Brooke to go to bed. Brooke nodded at me as they left the room. I wasn't sure what that meant but she didn't seem to be as hostile towards me as I thought she would be.

"You ready to go?" J asked, without as much as a

glance in my direction. He was already heading towards the front door, my answer clearly not even important.

I didn't bother answering him, simply followed him out to his bike. Without uttering a word to each other, we rode back to the clubhouse and my resolve to stay away from him strengthened.

10

Jason

I COLLAPSED ONTO the bed, thankful as fuck the day was over. I didn't have it in me to bother heading home so I crashed in my room at the clubhouse. The ride home from Coffs Harbour had been long, probably because I couldn't concentrate with my dick doing the fucking happy dance that Madison's tits and pussy were pressed tight to me. It had been just over four hours of torturous bliss; her on the back of my bike again was something I had never thought would happen, but I was sure as fuck glad it did.

And then she had gone and pissed me off, and I'd said stuff I wished I could take back because I didn't really mean it. Fuck, I had really hurt her. I could see it in her eyes and hear it in her voice. Maybe it was my way of pushing her away. There was that old familiar pull to her and I wasn't sure it was a good idea to even consider getting close again. But, fuck, I just had to be in the same room as her, and I wanted to touch her and bury my dick as far in her as I could.

Watching her get into an argument with Scott and then listening to her tell me off had been both infuriating and a relief. It was good to see the old Madison back. She had slowly disappeared on me after the incident with Rob all those years ago, and the drinking only made it worse. It had fucking killed me to see her lose her spark. Madison was the kind of woman who didn't let any man walk all over her, and after we broke up, I'd been horrified watching her allow Nix to control her.

The night I found her beaten up was one of the worst nights of my life. If I hadn't let her go, hadn't given up on us, she wouldn't have ended up with Nix and he wouldn't have laid a finger on her. I had sworn death after that and had meant it. Scott and her father had been with me on this, but then club politics got in the way. If we'd followed through on our threat, it would have ended in all-out war between Storm and the Black Deeds, and our club wasn't ready for that back then. We'd spent the last two years getting our shit in order, getting ready to strike and take the fucker down. Getting Madison out of the picture had been an important part of this plan, even though I hadn't agreed with it at first. I'd wanted her back with me, where she belonged, but Scott had ordered me to make sure she left town. I'd done this all right; I'd killed any love she might have had left for me the day I told her to get the fuck out; the day I told her I didn't love her anymore.

Seeing the difference in her, knew we'd done the right thing. When she left, she'd been drowning in alcohol. I hated watching her do that to herself; I felt useless, unable to make her see what she was doing. My mother had done the same thing and it was like watching re-runs of shitty television; seeing the same old crap over and over, hating it more each time. Madison finally had her life together so it made the last couple of years' worth it, even if she didn't want anything to do with me.

I was almost asleep when Scott bashed on my door. "J, need you, man."

"Fuck! Really?" I yelled back. It was just after midnight and I was wiped.

"Yeah, need you to check on Madison," he replied.

Shit, just the sound of her name stirred me. I sat up and reached for my boots. "Hang on, be there in a minute."

Scott was pacing at the bar when I found him. He looked up and I was instantly alert. Scott was known for keeping his shit together, but he looked stressed.

"What's happened?" I asked.

He stopped pacing and raked his fingers through his hair. "Davey was keeping an eye on Madison but she ditched him. I've got no fuckin' idea where she is."

"Jesus fucking Christ!" I roared. "What the fuck is wrong with these dickheads? They can't even do a simple job."

Scott nodded in agreement. "Yeah, brother. That leaves you and me to find her. I don't trust anyone else."

"Got any leads at all?" I asked, hoping like hell that he did.

"No. This is a fuckin' nightmare because Nix has shown back up in town."

Fuck! Not what I wanted to hear. Needing to lash out at

something, anything, I turned around and punched the closest wall. Davey was fucking lucky that he wasn't in sight because I would have pounded him if he was.

Scott's phone rang, and while he answered it, I mentally filed through a list of Madison's old friends trying to work out where she might have gone. I came up short because she had wiped a lot of her friends when she was with Nix.

"Right, Madison might be at Hyde's." He slipped his phone into his pocket. "Let's go." He headed towards the front door.

I reached out and grabbed his arm, turning him around to face me. "You're fucking kidding me, right? Not even twenty-four hours home and she starts fucking drinking again?" I was pissed. Pissed at her, at Nix, and at the whole fucking situation. Hyde's was her old favourite drinking ground, and the last place I thought she would be.

Scott pulled his arm back and snapped at me, "How 'bout you give her a break? She might surprise the fuck out of you."

"Yeah, and she might fucking not." I fixed an angry glare on him. "I've lived with, and buried an alcoholic, motherfucker. I know how they work." I pushed past him and stormed outside. I was in a really bad mood, and when we found Madison, she wasn't going to know what fucking hit her, especially if we found her drinking.

～

AN HOUR LATER, we still hadn't found her. I was surprised but relieved not to find her at Hyde's; I didn't want to think about how I would have reacted if we had found her there. We visited some of her old friends, and pissed them all off by waking them up. But none of them had seen her or heard from her. Scott was ropeable and I was pretty close. Then we got a call from Griff; Madison had shown up at the clubhouse.

We made our way back, and as I stormed into the bar, I noted her tear-stained face, but paid no attention to it. I grabbed her by the arm and pulled her towards me. "Have you any fucking idea how worried we have been?" I yelled at her.

She crumbled into my arms and started to sob. My reaction was automatic; I held her close, running my hand over her hair, trying to soothe her. The anger left me, and I felt the need to make everything all right for her. "Where were you, baby?" I asked.

She didn't answer me and Scott barked at her, "Answer us, Madison. Where the fuck were you?"

I looked up at him, anger burning through me again, but this time directed at him. "Back the fuck off, brother. In fact, everyone get the fuck out of here," I bellowed, and when no one moved, I added, "Now!"

People started moving out of the room and Scott stood there glaring at me for a minute or so, and then he left too.

I pulled back a little from Madison, to look in her eyes, "Baby, what's going on? Talk to me."

Her eyes slid to mine and the heartache I saw there stabbed me in the fucking heart. "I went to Bec's house. I just sat outside and remembered stuff, you know, the good times we'd had, even the bad. J, I miss her so much. I can't believe she's gone. Even though we weren't friends anymore, I always thought we'd patch it up." Tears streamed down her face.

"Fuck." I didn't know what else to say. I was useless at this shit, so I just pulled her close again and held her, letting her get it all out.

Eventually, she unwrapped her arms from me and wiped the tears from her face. "Sorry. I guess it is really hitting me, now that I'm back here," she apologised.

"No need to say sorry. But the next time you want to take off, for fuck's sake, let one of us know where you're going. Okay?"

"Okay."

I doubted she meant it. Madison did whatever she wanted, whenever she wanted. "Nix is back, apparently. That's why we were all so pissed at you. Plus, and you might find this hard to believe, we all care about you."

She stayed quiet for a moment, appraising me, and then she offered, "Thank you. I'm going to bed now. Goodnight."

She left and I stood in stunned silence. She had surprised the fuck out of me and I hated to admit it, but my heart was starting to want what my dick wanted.

11

MADISON

I WOKE UP the next morning feeling low. Remembering Bec the previous night had been hard and I was thankful that J had been there for me when I got back. That was a difficult thing to admit to myself. I just wanted to hate him and not have anything to do with him, but then he had to go and be nice to me. And the things he did to my body. God, I was so messed up about him. He'd been back in my life for less than a week, yet there I was, wanting him all over again.

I decided to put thoughts of J aside and focus on my plan to move back. First order of business would be to call Gina and let her know I wouldn't be coming back to work. Thank goodness I'd saved some money to get me through until I found a new job.

I grabbed my phone and dialled her number. "Hi, babe," she answered.

"Hey, Gina. I have some bad news for you." I decided to get straight to the point.

"You're not coming back, are you?"

"I'm so sorry to do this at such short notice but no, I am staying here. My friend's kid needs me," I answered her, really regretting having to do this to her.

"I understand, and actually wondered if you might end up staying. You're just lucky I love you; otherwise, I would send Zane after you," she threatened, but I heard the smile in her voice.

I shuddered at that thought. Zane was Blake and Gina's brother, and a man you didn't mess with. I'd only met him a few times and he scared the living shit out of me. I never asked Gina or Blake much about him because I really just didn't want to know who or what he was.

We chatted a bit more and I promised to visit her often before hanging up. I scrolled through my phone and hit Blake's number.

"Baby girl, how are you?" he said as he answered his phone.

"Have you got a few hours?" I asked, jokingly.

He chuckled. "That bad? Do you need me to come and sort shit out?"

"I appreciate that, but no. You've got your own things to take care of and I'm a big girl; it's time for me to sort out everything I walked away from years ago."

"Yeah, I guess it is. How's J? Still being a caveman?" I could hear the annoyance in his voice.

"J will always be a caveman. It's just who he is. I'm so confused about him, Blake." I decided that perhaps a guy's perspective might be insightful.

"In what way?"

I hadn't ever told my friends much about my relationship with J so I figured it was time to open up a bit, especially if I wanted advice. "I left Brisbane because he told me to. We'd been broken up for about six months but I thought we were going to get back together, and then he told me he didn't love me anymore and that I needed to leave. He was the one who lined my job up with Gina, through another club member who knew her, I think. He said I needed space from the club to get my drinking sorted. He broke my heart but I thought I was over him. Now I'm not so sure. I don't know what the fuck to make of it all."

"Talk to him. But you need to work out what you want first," he said.

"You're such a guy, Blake. You make it sound so easy." I sighed. Why did guys think that every situation was so black and white?

"Well, why do women make everything so hard?" he asked.

"We don't!"

He laughed. "Yeah, you do. We'll have to agree to disagree. Just promise me you'll talk to him."

"I'll try, but all we seem to do is argue, so it might not be as easy as you suggest."

"Show him a bit of leg. It'll shut him up for a minute and give you time to talk," he suggested.

It was my turn to laugh. "Great plan, maybe I'll flash my tits too, you know, to give me even more time."

"Settle down, you want him to be coherent, don't you?

Flashing your tits will send all the blood from his brain to his dick. Take my advice, no tits."

"Okay, legs it is. Now, did Serena tell you that I'm moving back here?" I asked, and we talked some more about my move and what was going on in his life before ending the call. I knew it wouldn't be long before one of us made the trip to visit the other; we couldn't go too long without needing to see each other.

"MADISON, GOOD TO SEE YOU, BABE."

I'd made my way downstairs to the club bar. Turning towards the voice I knew so well, I threw myself at him. "Nash, I've missed you," I said as we hugged.

"You're still as fucking hot as you were last time I saw you," he said, looking me up and down.

"And you're still as fucking pervy as you were last time I saw you." I slapped him on the arm, all the while smiling at him.

He grinned that wicked smile I remembered and shrugged. "Yep, and still the hot ass you missed out on when you chose that fucker, J."

Now it was my turn to grin at him. "Didn't know what I was getting myself into there, did I? And to think I could have had you."

"Fucker's still got a hard-on for you, too. He's got pussy anywhere he wants but none of it does what you did for him," Nash said, shaking his head.

What the fuck? My mouth dropped open in shock, and I was about to quiz him when we were interrupted.

"Nash," J's voice boomed from behind me and I spun around to see him shooting daggers at Nash. Oh, God, I felt bad for Nash. He and J had always had a hard relationship and J had never taken kindly to Nash's flirting with me.

Nash leaned over and whispered in my ear, "Looks like it's time for me to get out of here." He kissed my cheek, winked at me and said, "Later, sweet thing." He lifted his chin at J and then left us alone.

J walked toward me with a fierce determination and my stomach fluttered. He had a feral look in his eyes and, fuck, it did things to me. "He's right," he said as he stopped right in front of me; so close, too close.

My brain couldn't function properly when he was so close to me. His smell engulfed me and I wanted to reach out to touch him, taste him. It was too much and I tried to push him away, but he grabbed my hand and pulled me closer. Our bodies touched and I felt it not only physically, but also in my soul. He bent and breathed in the scent of me too. "Fuck, you smell so fucking good." He groaned as he pressed even closer so that I could feel his erection against me.

My body took over and I reached my hand up to wrap around his neck while lifting my lips to his. Our eyes met and I could see the same need in his that I had. His arms encircled me, and he ran one hand over my ass before tilting his head and finally kissing me. God, it felt so good. With his hands roaming over me, his lips and tongue devouring me, a thrill ran through me. A deep and uncontrollable urge took over and I pushed myself right into him; I needed to get as close as I possibly could. My hands gripped his hair and I plunged my tongue into his mouth, kissing him hard. He groaned again and that sound set me off even more. Fuck, I couldn't get enough of him. It had been so long without his touch. I needed more.

J suddenly pushed me away and raked his hand through his hair, looking utterly torn. "Fuck!" he sputtered.

I was still trying to get my wits about me, my brain scrambling from that kiss, and I was confused about what Nash had said. Keeping my mouth shut would never get me answers. Looking J dead in the eyes, I demanded, "What did Nash mean by that?"

"Exactly what he fucking said, babe."

I scrunched my eyebrows together, still not getting it. "You still want me?"

"Jesus, how many other ways do you need it said? I never stopped wanting you," he replied in a gruff voice.

I threw my hands up in the air. "Well, why the fuck did you tell me to leave?" I yelled, my anger growing.

"You needed to get out, get away from the club and all the shit that had gone down. You needed to deal with your drinking and I thought you could do that better somewhere else."

"No! You don't get to say that. That's a load of shit, J. Tell me the real fucking reason." Deep down, I knew there had to be more. I always had but it was easier just to let it sit there in my subconscious rather than trying to work it out.

He was exasperated by my outburst and I momentarily wondered if I had pushed him too far. "I had to. The club..." he paced wildly, "...the club needed you gone."

"What?" I held my breath, waiting for his explanation. None of this was making any sense .

He stopped pacing and fixed pained eyes on me; he was calmer now too, like he had settled something in his mind. "Baby, you need to know that I never wanted you to leave. But after what happened with Nix, the club swore blood, and we needed you gone to be able to do that. There was no way Nix would give you up if you were still here so we arranged for that job with Gina and sent you away." He came closer to me again and reached for my hand, holding it. "The only reason I told you that I didn't love you anymore was to make sure you would leave. I did it for your safety. You've gotta know that. I did love you. I still fucking do."

"No! You said you didn't want me. I moved on!" I shouted, getting in his face. I was really angry now. How dare the club control my life like that, and how dare he give me up for the fucking club.

"Are you listening to me, Madison? Did you hear me say—"

I cut him off and shoved at him. "It's too fucking late, J. You gave up on us. You took the club's side like you always did. I didn't need revenge on Nix. I just needed out from him and I *was* out."

J glowered at me and took a step back. "Let's get one thing straight, right now. I did not give up on us. And I did not fucking take the club's side every time," he thundered. "But babe, you've gotta understand that when the club rules like they did, I got no choice."

I stabbed a finger at him. "And that right there is the fucking problem! We never had a chance with the club controlling us."

"Madison, the club ruled and I followed through. Jesus, babe, you grew up in the club, you know how it works. Our problems weren't to do with the club."

"Well, the club had a lot to do with them. The club and its way of dealing with shit."

He cocked his head to the side and studied me for a moment. "What exactly are we talking about now?" he asked, and I wished I had kept my mouth shut. I didn't want to have this conversation today.

"J, this conversation is pointless—"

He came closer to me again, his breathing ragged and his face a picture of anger. Bending down to meet my eyes, he spat, "I fucking tell you that I still love you, and you tell me this conversation is pointless?"

And just like that, the anger seeped out of me and all I felt was desire. J had invaded my space and my senses again, and telling me he still loved me only heightened my craving for him. I knew I needed to get out of here. I couldn't think straight when he was so close. I really needed to sort through my conflicting thoughts and feelings.

"I'm waiting for an answer, Madison. Is this conversation pointless?"

"I don't know, J, okay. I need some time to think," I finally answered him.

He stood up straight, his eyes intense and focused on mine. He took a moment and then said, "I'll give you some time. But then we talk. And babe, we will talk about every fucking thing we should have talked about two years ago."

With that, he turned and left me alone; alone to contemplate the conversation that we would finally be having. He was absolutely right. There were things that should have been said all those years ago; things that I still found hard to even think about, let alone talk about.

Shit.

But first, I needed to sort out the mess of feelings I was having about J. Why the fuck couldn't life ever be easy?

12

Madison

THE DAY passed fairly uneventfully after my run in with J. He left with Scott and some of the other guys to take care of something. I wasn't sure what it was they were doing but then again, I was never privy to that sort of information. And, yeah, it pissed me off. That was something that J never understood. He never shared club business with me, unlike some of the other club members who talked stuff through with their old ladies. I had wanted to be involved in J's life fully and that meant club life as well. I didn't expect to be told everything, but to be told nothing kind of hurt. It made me feel like I was only a part of some of J's life.

Hanging out at the clubhouse for most of the morning, I caught up with friends I hadn't seen in years. I loved that aspect of club life, the social side. These were my people; I had grown up here and felt totally comfortable. I loved living in Coffs Harbour but there was something peaceful about coming home to where I was accepted and loved without reservation.

After lunch, I headed to visit my mum. My parents lived about twenty minutes away so one of the guys took me. As we pulled up to the house, I was hit with the memories of growing up. Mum and Dad had given Scott and I a good life. We had been surrounded by lots of love in the form of club family. I remembered tons of get togethers with the boys and their families; parties, barbeques, you name it, my mum was always organising something. My dad may have been the club president, but my mother played a huge part in keeping it all together and running smoothly. I didn't know how aware she was of the day-to-day business of the club but I truly believed that she was the strong woman who stood behind my father and supported him in everything he did.

Sharon Cole was a woman who most people tried not to mess with. She was a hard-as-nails, straight-up, ballsy woman who loved fiercely, and lived and breathed Storm. Her father had been a member of Storm, and she too had grown up in the life. She had met my father when he joined the club and the rest was history. They had been through a lot and had built Storm up to be the club it was today: a force to be reckoned with. Storm had a reputation for getting the job done and it was a club that others didn't fuck with, although that reputation had really only come about over the last few years.

Even though I hadn't had much to do with Storm since I left, I had heard whisperings from friends about the lengths the club would go to in order to protect its business dealings, its members and their loved ones. As much as I wasn't aware of within the club, I wasn't naïve; I had seen enough to know there was a lot of violence involved, and it seemed that this had only intensified. I struggled with that when I dated J; he had sometimes come home bloodied and bruised, and when I asked about it, he always told me it was club business and I didn't need to know. Thinking about my mother, I wondered how she dealt with that side of Storm. We had never talked about it but perhaps it was something I needed to ask her; perhaps learning how to deal with it would help me move past what had happened with Rob.

I never knew just what J was capable of until Rob. I shuddered thinking about it, but the thing was, I had to think about it. I had pushed it to the deep recesses of my mind for too long. It had everything to do with why J and I broke up, so in order for me to start sorting through my feelings about him, I needed to work through that first.

"So, I hear you're staying," Mum said as she made us coffee. She had been happy to see me and I could hear the relief in her voice.

I smiled; it was so good to see her. "Yes." I took a moment to get the words out right. "I haven't wanted to come back because I wasn't sure how I would cope with everything here. I thought that seeing J again would he hard and, to be honest, I was trying to get away from the club. But you know what? I think I've missed the club and even though he's pissing me off, I'm okay with being around J."

She nodded. "You were in a pretty bad way when you left, Maddy, but I think you just needed that time away to get your head together. It's done you good, honey."

"I want to stay so I can watch out for Crystal, but being here with you now, I realise I've really missed you, even if you are overbearing sometimes," I said with a cheeky smile.

Mum laughed. "I've been good lately, haven't I?" she asked.

"Yeah, Mum, you have. And I need you to let me do things my way if I've any chance of starting over here and keeping my shit together. Okay?"

She held up her hands. "Okay, okay. So, what's your plan? Do you want to move in here with us until you sort yourself out? I know your father would love to have you here."

"He's got a funny way of showing it. He bit my head off yesterday."

"He is very stressed at the moment with what is happening with Nix. Honey, he's been worried about you and, yeah, pissed off with you. He just wanted you home where he knew you were safe and all you did was fight it. He and Scott have been constantly arguing about you and I've got to say, it's been pretty hard living with him the last little while. So, I am really happy you are home."

"What do you mean they've been arguing about me?" I asked, having no clue what she could possibly mean.

"Your father would have just come and dragged you

home, nothing would have stopped him. But Scott stood up to him and argued that it had to be your decision. He understands how hard it's been for you, and he was so proud of you for quitting drinking; he just didn't want you to go backwards."

Well, fuck me. Scott was actually on my side. News to me. "Men! I can't fucking work them out," I said, totally exasperated with it all.

"Join the club, but I'll tell you one thing, and you make sure you listen closely. Scott and your father love you and will do anything for you. This vendetta against Nix started after he beat you, and it has only gotten worse since then. It's put a lot of pressure on Storm and they've copped that. For you. So, you need to cut them some slack and start working with them rather than against them."

"The problem is that they never give me the full story. You know what they're like—"

She cut me off, "Yes, I know exactly what they're like, Madison, but the difference between you and me is that I trust them. I know in my gut that everything they're doing is for us and for the club. I don't need to know the details, but you seem hell bent on having to know every little thing. And you haven't ever given them your complete trust. Dare I say it, but I think that's where a lot of your problems with J come from too; you didn't trust him."

"How can I trust any of them when they don't trust me enough to tell me stuff?" I argued.

My mother sighed; that sigh I had grown up with that told me she was becoming frustrated with me. "Honey, it's their way. The club way. It's what their fathers did and their fathers before them probably; it's all they've ever known and it's drilled into them when they join. What happens in the club stays in the club. And if you can't live with that, you should never date another member again."

My natural reaction to all of this would normally be to continue arguing but I decided that perhaps it was time to start listening to my mother. She'd been living this life for a long time and knew what she was on about. I'd been fighting these ways for so long, yet it got me nowhere. So, I took a deep breath and asked her a question. "How do you live with the shit that goes on? How do you deal, knowing what Dad is capable of?"

She didn't skip a beat. "We're all capable of bad stuff, Maddy, but the shit they do is done for a reason. We've got a lifestyle that needs protecting, and your dad and the boys aren't afraid to protect it or us. I deal with that by choosing to love your father unconditionally and I make no apologies for it. When you really love a person, you trust them, and believe in them and everything they do." She cocked her head and gave me a quizzical look. "Are you thinking of getting back with J? Is that what all this is about?"

"I don't know what's happening with J. What I do know is that I need to find a way to be okay with what they do." And yeah, I also needed to decide if I wanted to be with J again, but I was keeping that to myself.

"Nothing's fucking happening with J." We both jumped as the snarl of Nix's voice swept through the room.

I screamed just as one of his guys grabbed me from behind and covered my mouth with his hand. Fear sliced through me, and the stench of sweat and tobacco overwhelmed me. Nausea hit and then the blackness took over.

∼

WHEN I CAME TO, I was tied to a chair and Nix stood in front of me, leaning down into my face. His hot, acrid breath filled my senses. His eyes were crazy; fuck, he was crazy. Mad. Demented.

Panic gripped my gut. I knew in that instant that I was as good as dead.

He ran a calloused finger down my cheek. "Madison, you came back to me."

Oh, God. He really was whacked in the head if he thought that. I didn't say anything, just maintained eye contact with him.

He stood up straight and my eyes followed him. He looked to his right, and I realised that my mother was also here, tied to a chair. She had tape covering her mouth and blood coming from her head. I was lucky to avoid all that. Her eyes were closed and she was slumped in her chair.

Nix nodded at a guy who was near my mum. A silent command flowed between them, and the guy hurried off. My foggy brain slowed my thinking and I gave up wondering what that was all about.

Nix turned his attention back to me. "I've missed you, Madison. Bec kept me company for a while, but she could never replace you or what we had. That bitch tried to fuck me over." He was rambling, and then he laughed shrilly.

"She got what she fucking deserved in the end." His eyes glinted. he was terrifying me, just from his body language.

I didn't want to talk to him, but I couldn't stop myself; I just hope my voice didn't quiver, giving away my fear. "What are you going to do to us, Nix?" I needed to know.

"I haven't quite worked out what I will do with you, but your mother is an unnecessary burden to us, wouldn't you say? She wouldn't stop yelling at me before, so I had to fucking knock her out. I don't need the headache," he replied. Nausea hit me at the thought of him killing my mum.

"Let her go and I'll do whatever you say," I frantically tried to negotiate with him.

He threw his head back and laughed. Then his face contorted into an evil mask and he sneered, "You'll do whatever the fuck I say anyway, bitch. I'm not fucking bargaining with you for anything."

I hated him, but hated myself more for letting him into my life. Because of my past actions, my mother's life was in danger and there was not a fucking thing I could do about it.

Jason

MY FIST CONNECTED with the asshole's cheek and blood went flying. "I can keep this up, motherfucker, until you tell us where Nix is," I warned.

He landed on his ass and looked up at me through feral

eyes. "Go to fucking hell," he snarled and spat blood onto the ground.

Scott reefed him up from behind and held him in front of me. "Take another shot, brother," he invited.

I had enough and was way past pissed off. We'd been going at this for over half an hour and it was time to move it along. I pulled out my gun and stepped closer, putting it to his head. "I'll make this real fucking easy for you. Start fucking talking," I thundered.

He glared at me but saw him weakening under the pressure so when he again refused to give up the information, I aimed the gun at his foot and shot. I took great pleasure in the blood this caused. I craved their fucking blood.

"Motherfucker!" he screamed in agony, and tried to struggle out of Scott's hold.

Oh, yeah, asshole, I was just getting started. I lifted the gun and aimed it at his other foot, and was just about to shoot when he yelled, "Wait! I'll tell you. Just fucking stop shooting!"

"Well, hurry the fuck up. We don't have all day," I bellowed at him, trying to create some fucking urgency for him to deliver the details.

"Warehouse on Woods," he grumbled, and the adrenaline coursed through me with this new information. We were finally going to get that cocksucker. He'd been one step ahead of us for too fucking long; it was time to take him down.

Scott flashed me an evil grin. "Time to rock and roll, brother."

TEN MINUTES later we were heading to the warehouse. Scott had called Marcus, and he was rounding up the boys to meet us there. I was fired up to take Nix down. Finally, it had been a long time coming. When Marcus had put a stop to our original plan two years earlier, I had been pissed off, but he'd managed to convince me it was for the best. We had all worked hard the last couple of years to build Storm up, and in that time, Nix had gone even more rogue. He had taken over the Presidency of Black Deeds and was now pissing all over that club pursuing his own agenda. Killing Bec and her son had been the final nail in his coffin as far as we were concerned, and I was fucking ecstatic when Marcus had given the order to put him to ground.

My mind wandered to Madison. Fuck, I was glad she was back but it was stirring shit up in me that I thought was over and done with. I still loved her and had always known that, but I figured that relationship was in the past. I was no longer so sure. I wanted her. But I wasn't convinced we could deal with the past and move on from it. Madison seemed to have a lot of issues with it all. Fuck, but I wanted her.

I put thoughts of her aside to focus on the job at hand. Following Scott to the warehouse, I noted there were only a couple of bikes parked outside; hopefully, this meant Nix didn't have much company.

While we waited for Marcus and the boys to turn up, Scott asked, "What's the deal with you and Madison?"

"Not sure, brother. Your sister has a fucking mind of

her own and I'm not sure I'll ever get through it."

He chuckled. "You wouldn't have it any other way. A submissive bitch wouldn't stand a chance with you," he said and then his face turned serious. "Don't fuck her over. She's not as tough as she likes to make out."

"I hear you," I agreed. And I did. Madison liked to present a tough front but underneath it all she was pretty sensitive, and perhaps that was something I hadn't paid enough attention to when we were together. It was certainly something I had figured out as our relationship had spiralled into a shit storm of hurt, anger and resentment. Too little, too fucking late though.

Scott nodded at me. "Good." He then turned his head to acknowledge Marcus who was walking towards us.

He brought ten of the boys with him and we quickly discussed the best course of action. We split up: half going to the back, and the rest to the front of the warehouse. I was fucking itching to get in there and I pulled my gun out, ready to go.

Scott stormed through the door and we found Nix with three of his guys in there. But, fuck me, he was one step ahead of us again. Scott lifted his finger to indicate for us all to stop but I saw fucking red and wasn't sure I could stop.

Nix chuckled, eyes glinting with sinister fucking glee. "Looks like you're just in time for the party, boys."

I powered past Scott, intent on killing Nix but he grasped my arm and yanked me back. "Now's not the fuckin' time, J. Be smart, brother," he hissed.

"I don't know how you can be so fucking calm about this! He's got our fucking family there," I barked.

Nix had Scott's mother and Madison tied up, guns trained on them, and my heart was fucking pounding in my chest. Scott wanted me to be smart but as far as I could see, it was time to stop thinking and start fucking doing. It appeared that Marcus had the same idea as me. He came thundering through the back entrance and barrelled into Nix, knocking him to the ground. I took that as my cue to follow suit and fired my gun at the asshole who had Madison. I hit him dead in the eyes and he dropped like the piece of shit he was.

"Fuck!" Scott bellowed and gave the signal to the boys to get in it.

Marcus was busy with Nix and I had no doubt he could hold his own until we got the others under control, so I charged straight for the guy closest to me and swung my fist at him. I connected but he took a swing back and the crack across my cheek fucking hurt, but it didn't stop me. With all this adrenaline coursing through my system, I didn't think much could. We continued to trade punches but he was one tough motherfucker and just kept coming back for more.

Just when I thought I had him, a shot rang out and I turned to see that the VP of Black Deeds, Bullet, had arrived, along with about six other members. "Enough!" he yelled, and his guys all focused their guns on us.

Fuck.

Bullet was a nasty piece of work, and he appeared to be in a murderous mood going by the look on his face, and his tense body. He spoke at Marcus, "Let Nix go." He trained his gun on Madison. "Or I shoot her."

Marcus didn't hesitate. He shoved Nix towards Bullet.

Nix stumbled, but turned and attempted to punch Marcus, who saw it coming, ducked and then straightened, grabbing Nix by the throat.

Bullet stalked over to them and ripped Nix away from Marcus. "Fucking leave it, Nix," he growled. "This shit is done."

Nix turned his dark eyes on Bullet and seethed, "Watch your fucking mouth, VP. This shit isn't done till I say it is, and it's not fucking done."

Bullet nodded at one of their guys who turned his gun from our people and aimed it at Nix. "The club says it's done," Bullet asserted, and the guy pulled the trigger.

Stunned, I watched as Nix slumped to the floor. Never in a million years had I expected that they would take their own president out. But, it was possibly the best move they could have made.

My eyes shot to Madison and I took in her alarm. Fuck, this needed to be over but I had no clue where Bullet was taking it.

"Right, you get your guys out of here and this is done. No fucking retribution for anything Nix did; he wasn't backed by the club for any of that shit," Bullet said to Marcus.

Marcus considered what he had said, giving both Scott and me a quick glance. Scott lifted his chin, indicating his consent and I followed suit. We didn't want a war with Black Deeds; it had only ever been Nix who we were after, and that had been taken care of. I was fucking pissed though. I'd wanted to draw his death out and fucking make him suffer. I'd wanted to be the cause of his blood pouring from his body.

Turning back to Bullet, Marcus agreed and then raised his hand in the air, circling his finger and pointing at the door. He grabbed Sharon and I headed towards Madison, who Scott had untied.

I held her face between my hands and searched her eyes. "You okay, baby?" I asked.

She kept her shit together and nodded. "Yeah," she replied and then, with an emotion I couldn't quite figure out, "Take me home, J." Her hands covered mine and she grasped them both pulling them down to our sides. We stood there for a moment like that, her eyes no longer cold towards me but rather, there was a heat to her stare. And it fucking hit me in the belly and then, of course, my dick did his happy dance again. I growled and nodded, leading her out to my bike, not even giving Bullet, Marcus or any of the boys a second glance.

I was fucking taking Madison home, and no fucker was getting in my way.

13

Madison

J WAS ON a mission and I was going with it. I was letting myself feel again. After shutting my feelings down for so long, to allow myself go there again was electric. My body buzzed, my mind dancing with the possibilities, and my desire for J was in fucking overdrive. I needed to have him. *Now.*

Any doubts I had been having about how he felt had been erased when I saw the raw emotion playing on his face when he saw me tied up by Nix. I never thought I'd see the day, but I was relieved when he'd killed that fucker standing over me. It was no secret that I struggled with the violence surrounding Storm, but my eyes had been opened and Mum was right; anything J did was for those he loved. Even what he had done to Rob. I was shitty at myself for taking so long to see this because it had kept me from J all this time. And I didn't want to be without him for one second longer.

I followed him wordlessly through his house into his bedroom, all the while holding his hand; I wasn't letting him go.

When we reached his room, he turned to me, and pulled me to him. Our eyes locked and I licked my bottom lip, drawing his attention to my mouth. I wrapped my hands around his neck letting my fingers thread through his hair and then pulled his face to mine. The minute our lips met, my core clenched and my brain became a scrambled mess. I needed this man like I had never needed another, and I pushed myself closer to him; I couldn't get close enough.

He groaned and reached his hands down to my ass and lifted me up so that my legs were wrapped around him. Next second, we were up against the wall, lips smashed together and his hands were under my top, searching for my breasts.

"Baby, you feel so good," he murmured as he rolled my nipple between his fingers.

"Fuck, J," I moaned, and then kissed him before pulling back away. "Why did we wait so long?" It wasn't really a question that required answering; more a statement of how much I wanted this right now.

"I don't fucking know, but don't think that you can stop me now, 'cause nothing will fucking stop me now. I'm yours and you're mine, always have been." He stared intently into my eyes when he spoke.

I nodded and smiled. "Yes," I said simply, and then a little more aggressively, "Now, fuck me."

He grinned, and then his lips were back on mine: hard, insistent. Gripping my ass, he turned and walked us to the bed, laying me down while he stood and watched me from hooded eyes.

"Take your clothes off, baby," he commanded and I didn't hesitate to obey.

I shimmied out of my jeans, lifted off my top and threw it on the floor, closely followed by my bra. Fuck, watching J watch me made me wetter than I already was. I couldn't resist playing with him a little. Running my hands over my tits, I pinched my nipples, and then reached one hand down into my panties and rubbed my clit. My eyes did not leave J, but his eyes roamed my body, first watching me touch my tits and then following my hand into my panties. He loved to watch, and I loved to be watched. I had forgotten how in sync we were.

"Taste yourself," he said as he reached down and unbuttoned his jeans.

He pulled his cock free and stroked it. All the time, his eyes remained on my pussy, eager for a show, so I dipped my finger into my wetness and then lifted it to my lips, sucking and licking. He stroked harder and a little faster, which only turned me on more. I moved to a kneeling position in front of him on the bed and pushed his jeans down; I wanted all barriers to J removed. Stepping out of them, he tugged off his shirt. J liked to go commando so he now stood naked in front of me and it was a fucking heavenly sight to behold.

I traced the ink on his chest, remembering the day he had it done. It was my name tattooed in an anchor and I was surprised and thrilled that he still had it. His hand cupped my chin and he tilted my face up to look at him while his other hand wrapped around mine that had been exploring his chest.

"Baby, it's always been you. Always. Tell me you believe that," he said, his voice husky.

"Yes, I believe it, J," I breathed out, full of love and desire. I reached my other hand up to his face and pulled him to me, kissing him deep and hard, before admitting, "And it's always been you. I thought this was done, but it's not, and I don't ever want it to be." I laid my heart bare before him and prayed he wouldn't fuck with it again; that he would treasure it and help me to finally put it back together.

"It won't ever be done. You and me, that's forever, and this time… this time I will do right by you. I thought I had always put you first, but today, seeing you there, fucking tied up… fuck, baby, today I realised that I would do anything for you. I won't make the mistakes I've made in the past."

And just like that, he had me. I was back where I should be. I was his. He had my heart again and it was time to give him my body. Briefly, I touched his ink again and then trailed my hand slowly down to his cock. He sucked in a breath as I took hold and moved my hand up and down the length of him, slow at first and then faster.

J suddenly gripped my hand and stopped me, a feral look on his face. "Feels so fucking good, but it's been too long without you, baby. I want this to last longer than a minute," he grunted.

My body flooded with warmth at his words and a tingle spread out from my heart. I was impatient to have him but his words hit my sweet spot, so I let him set the pace. Pulling away, laid back on the bed. Touching my pussy through my panties I enticed him. "It's all yours, J. You've just got to come and get it."

He wasted no time. He leant over me and ripped my panties off. Spreading my legs, he dipped his head between them. When his tongue hit my clit, I gripped the bed to steady myself, the firework of sensations within me leaving me gasping for breath and threatening to make me come undone. Growling with pleasure, the vibrations raced through me, sending a desperate need for more. I struggled to hold back, to let him continue this slow, maddening tease.

He continued to explore me with his tongue while his hands held my ass and positioned my legs over his shoulders. I tangled my fingers in his hair and tugged when the pressure built, grinding my pussy into his face. Fuck, I loved his mouth on me. When he pushed a finger inside, I gripped his hair hard; I was almost there. One finger became two and he pushed and swirled inside me until the pressure grew and I came in a glorious moment of ecstasy.

J lifted his head and untangled my legs from his shoulders. He moved up the bed until his face was over mine and he kissed me, the taste of my pussy in his mouth. I loved it when he tasted me and it sent me a little wild; I kissed him harder and moaned deep in my throat.

He kissed me back just as hard and then pulled away, chuckling, "You still like to taste your own pussy, babe?"

I entwined my leg around his, sliding my foot down his calf and pushed up so my sex touched his body. "Fuck, yeah." I grinned at him before reaching for his cock. "J, I need you in me. Now," I begged.

"You've no fucking idea how much I need to be in you, baby," he rasped, slamming his mouth onto mine, our lips and tongues melding perfectly together.

The kiss was electrifying and J only ended it so he could move his lips to my neck and then down to my breasts, where he sucked and nipped at my nipples. While I enjoyed the foreplay—his mouth on my nipples incredible—I was ready for him. Hell, I'd always been ready for him. I pushed at his head so he was looking up at me. "Now, J. I need you to fuck me, now," I demanded.

He pushed himself up and reached for his pants, grabbing a condom out of his wallet, eyes on me while he did this. I loved the desire I saw in those eyes and the heady feeling it gave me. Once he had the condom on, he came back to me for another hard and fast kiss. I wrapped both legs around him and finally, he entered me, slow at first and then he thrust all the way in.

Fuck!

J's cock filled me and he thrust in and out, in and out as he watched me, his breathing erratic. Every one of my nerve endings was on fire and I squeezed my eyes shut as the sensations shot through me.

"Eyes, babe," J grunted, and I snapped my eyes open. "Keep 'em on me," he ordered.

I raised my neck off the bed and flicked my tongue out to taste his lips and he bent his head a little and kissed me, plunging his tongue into my mouth. Holy hell, I never wanted to have sex with another man again. J was it for me. In truth, I'd always known this. My arms were already around him, but I clawed his back, trying to wrap myself closer around him while he pounded into me. And then my core contracted one last time before I shattered around him, coming hard. J wasn't far behind me, releasing a fierce grunt before he thrust as far and as hard as he could, before stilling as he came. Spent, his head fell next to mine and he lay on me.

We lay locked together, savouring the release and the joining. Reluctantly he rolled off me and stood, removing the condom and dealing with it before coming back to the bed and lying on his side next to me. He propped himself up on his elbow, resting his head on his hand and reached out to smooth my hair. No words were spoken while he gently caressed my face, and yet his actions spoke volumes.

Once our heavy breathing calmed, he spoke. "Your pussy, babe. It's mine."

"Really? And who says so?" I couldn't help but play with him and his cocky, territorial attitude, even though I wholeheartedly agreed with him.

He raised his eyebrows. "After that, you're gonna fucking argue?"

"Maybe I just like to have a say in these things."

"Yeah, baby. I remember." He rolled his eyes. "But let's settle this now. You and your pussy are mine. Yeah?"

I laughed. "Yeah, J. We're yours." I leaned over, and gave him a quick kiss.

"Thank fuck, babe," he said before pulling me close

and turning me so that we were spooning. "Now have a rest. It's been a long fucking day."

He didn't have to tell me twice. I was out fast, dreaming of a future with my man.

14

MADISON

A COUPLE OF hours later, I woke to the sound of J speaking in a hushed tone on his phone. He was sitting on the edge of the bed with his back to me, running a hand through his hair. I admired his back and the way his muscles rippled as his arm moved, including the Storm tattoo I had grown up with and knew so well from my father; it held so much meaning to me. I sighed. I was home. J was home, and Storm was home.

J finished his call and stood. He gave me a quick glance as he walked towards his bathroom; but no smile, just a serious, focused look.

Shit.

My insecurities flared up. Was he having second thoughts about us? Even after the "your pussy is mine" speech?

I got up and quickly dressed. I felt the need to be dressed if he was going to reject me now.

He came out of the bathroom and abruptly stopped when he took in my state of dress. "What the fuck, Madison? I thought we had this sorted. Why are you leaving?"

"I thought—" He shook his head, annoyed.

"Stop fucking analysing shit." He came to me and cupped my cheek, grazing my lips with his thumb. "I told you where I stand. What I want. Take that in, babe, and know it. Feel it. But you've gotta fucking stop over thinking everything 'cause there's gonna be times where I might not make sense and things might get messy. I need you to have faith in me, in us. Yeah?"

Shit. I was a neurotic bitch. *Note to self: calm that shit down.* "Yeah. But it might take me some time to get there so I need you to work with that. Okay?"

He nodded. "Done," he replied, and then smacked me on the ass. "Now, we've got to get to the clubhouse. Marcus is pissed at me, something about wanting to make sure you're okay, and then we've got some club business to deal with."

I was about to come back with a smartass reply regarding my father, but then I remembered the conversation with my mum today. I had opened my heart to J. Perhaps it was time to give my father another chance.

∼

Fifteen minutes later wc walked into the clubhouse and J

left me at the bar to search for Marcus. The bar was full of club members who appeared to be celebrating something, most likely Nix's death. Yeah, that was something to fucking celebrate. I smiled at them to let them know I was okay and went to find Mum.

She was in the kitchen making food, for what I was guessing was a full blown party, judging by the amount of food she had in there. "Hey, honey." She stopped what she was doing and searched my face. "You okay?" she asked.

"Yeah, and you?"

She waved her hand at me in a dismissive motion. "You know me, nothing fazes me." Yep, that was true. My mother was unflappable—a tough bitch who could get through any situation.

"Do you need help with all this food?" I asked, changing the conversation. I hated discussing my feelings; better just to get on and deal with it yourself rather than whining to anyone who would listen.

"Thanks, honey," she answered and, for the next hour, we worked together, getting all the boys and their families fed. News of Nix's demise had spread fast, and loved ones had shown up to celebrate the end of the club's battle with him. From what people told me, it had been a long, hard two years since I left. The club had put a lot of work into bringing him down and everyone was glad to see the end of this episode.

Just as Mum and I were finishing up in the kitchen, J wandered in. He hooked an arm around my waist and pulled me to him. "Your dad wants to see you, baby," he said and the tenderness in his voice made my stomach flutter. J didn't often do tender so it meant something to me; perhaps it indicated a change in the way he was approaching our new relationship.

I smiled up at him. "Where is he?" I asked, and he told me where to find him. "I won't be long," I promised, and gave him a quick kiss as I left the kitchen.

∼

I FOUND my father outside talking to some of the boys. He glanced up when he saw me coming, his jaw set, no smile in place, but I saw the relief that flickered across his face in that moment and noted his shoulders settle out of their tense hold.

"Madison," he addressed me, and waved the boys away so we could have some privacy.

He exuded an agitated vibe and I didn't want a confrontation so I silently waited for him to continue, not wanting to say something that might set him off. When dealing with Marcus Cole, it was best to let him do most of the talking.

"You're okay." He nodded, reassuring himself.

"Yes, Dad, I'm okay," I confirmed.

Another moment passed between us, with him deliberating over something and then he let out a huge breath, curved his palm around my neck and pulled me to him in a hug. "Thank fuck," he uttered softly.

Shit, first J going all sensitive on me and Dad too. And then, out of nowhere, everything slammed into me at once. Relief, gratitude, joy, anger; I felt it all and then some. It unfurled within me, and I was overwhelmed to the point of tears. I started crying and Dad's hand lightly brushed over my hair, soothing me, making me sob even harder.

We stayed like that for what felt like a long time: him calming me with soft reassurances and me clinging to him in a way I never had. I had needed him to be this father many times in my life and he had never come through for me, but that time, I felt a shift and it affected me. Letting my guard down a little was liberating.

Eventually, my tears dried up and I let go. "Thank you," I said quietly, looking up into his eyes to see a mixture of concern and love.

He nodded and brushed his thumbs across my cheeks, wiping away my tears. "Madison, I know you and I haven't always seen eye to eye, and I fuckin' know I can be an asshole sometimes, but I'm workin' on it. I'm sorry you and your mother were put in that situation today; that you had to witness what you did. And I'm fuckin' worried about you, worried that this will send you back to that hell you were in after that motherfucker beat the shit out of you."

Well, fuck me, Marcus Cole was going all emotional on me. It was time to put his mind at ease. "You don't need to worry about me, Dad. Yeah, that was a fucked-up situation, and seeing Nix killed was not on my bucket list, but you know what? I'm happy it's done because it means you guys can get back to concentrating on club business and we can all breathe easier now. And as far as me losing the plot? It's not going to happen. I'm stronger now and I have all of you to back me up. This time around, my eyes are wide open and I'm seeing everything in a different light," I assured him, and then, needing to lighten the mood, I winked at him and said, "I'm not good at asking for help, but I'm working on it, just like you're working on not being such an asshole."

He threw his head back and laughed, and it was so good to see my Dad loosen up a little. "Okay, sweetheart, it's a deal," he agreed. "Now, let's get back inside to the party. We've got some celebrating to do."

The party lasted into the early hours and I was exhausted by two a.m. It had been a great night though, catching up with everyone after being away for the past couple of years and watching the boys shed the tension they had obviously been feeling. Even Scott let loose a little and I watched with interest as he flirted with a woman I didn't know. This was out of character for him; to my knowledge, Scott didn't usually put the hard yards in with the ladies; he just scored whenever he felt the need.

As I watched him, he caught my eye and smiled. It was a dazzling smile, one that Scott didn't often bring out. He was far too serious, and shouldered too much responsibility as far as I was concerned. I smiled back and then went looking for J.

"There you are," he said as I walked into the pool room. The club had three pool tables and J could often be found in there.

I was taken aback by the woman who was next to J, leaning over the table getting ready to take her shot, tits falling everywhere and ass barely covered by her animal print mini skirt. J had obviously been about to help her take her shot and their closeness sent a rush of jealousy through me. My fists clenched, and my face flushed with a burning heat. It stopped me dead in my tracks and all clear headed thought escaped me. A primal need to stake out my territory took over, damn the consequences.

"What the fuck?" I snapped at J.

Irritation spread across J's face and he stepped away from the skank and came towards me. "You're kidding, right?" he demanded, grabbing me by the arm and pulling me to the side.

I yanked my arm out of his grip. "No, I'm not fucking kidding!" I yelled at him, but my eyes were focused solely on the chick who was now looking me up and down as if I was the shit on the bottom of her shoes. "Who is she, J?"

His lips pinched together and I could tell he was fighting to remain calm. "She's no one, and you need to settle the fuck down," he warned me.

My head jerked back to look at him. "And you need to stop telling me what to do."

We glared at each other, neither saying a thing, but my mind was racing. How dare he tell me to settle down! I threw my hands in the air and madly declared, "I'm out of here. I need some space."

I turned and stalked out of the room, giving the skank a filthy glare on my way. Fucking club whores; they were all the same and I couldn't believe that J would let one drape herself all over him on the day we got back together.

Having no idea where I was going, I just kept walking and eventually found myself in J's room upstairs. I was mentally and physically exhausted from the day, but I needed a shower so I undressed and submersed myself under the steaming, hot water, letting it wash away the heaviness I was feeling.

Having not been in a relationship for the last two years,

I had enjoyed the peace of not having to work my way through shit like that. My relationship with J had always been a little volatile; it was the only aspect of it that I wished was different. Something had to give, to change if we were going to make it work this time. I just didn't know if either of us was capable of that.

As I was contemplating all this, J's ragged breathing engulfed the room and I turned to see him standing outside the shower. His wild eyes were on me, raking over my body with an intense passion that shot heat straight to my core and sent whatever thoughts I was having straight out of my mind. All I could think about was having J, having his cock in me again. He lifted his shirt over his head and discarded it, and then did the same to his shoes and jeans. I watched every movement intently, my hand snaking down to my clit to massage it while his body was revealed to me. Once he was naked, he opened the shower door and stepped in next to me, his body filling the small space. I continued touching myself and reached my other hand down to take hold of his cock and started stroking. J was hard and ready, and he emitted a groan with my movement.

Slipping his hands around me he ran them over my ass and pulled me closer to him, dipping his head to catch my mouth in a hard, forceful kiss. I kept massaging myself, circling and dipping my finger in my wet folds with one hand, while my other one ran up and down his cock. Our kiss became desperate, our breathing more erratic until J broke away to move his lips down my body, sucking, kissing, licking me on my neck and breasts. His hands were on my ass, my stomach, my tits and finally they were where I wanted them, where I needed them; he took over my pussy and began finger fucking me.

Fuck! It was almost more than I could take. The sensations shooting through my body were electric; J was fucking electric, and although I was overwhelmed by him, I also couldn't get enough. I started to climb up his body, the need to have him inside me taking over, desperate for his cock. He withdrew his fingers from my pussy and moved his hands to my ass, helping lift me up and then moved me so that I was leaning up against the shower wall. I wrapped my legs and arms around him, my hands gripping the back of his neck. Needing his mouth on mine, I took it, plunging my tongue in. I moaned with pleasure. He felt so fucking good. I would never get enough of him.

"Baby, I'm gonna fuck you now but I don't have a condom," he grunted between kisses.

"I'm clean," I managed to get out, not wanting him to stop; not ever stop.

"Good, me too," he uttered before thrusting in me hard and fast, to the hilt.

"Fuck!" I cried out. "Don't fucking stop, J. Fuck me hard," I demanded.

He didn't need further coaxing. He rammed into me repeatedly, our faces mashed side by side, our breathing hard and heavy while we each took what we needed. The rhythmic slapping of our bodies and our grunts were the only noises in the room and it turned me on even more. J began to move even faster with his thrusts and I felt it build; the divine pleasure intensifying until my pussy tightened and clenched and the release hit me, exploding throughout me, and I screamed with satisfaction.

"Fuck, baby," he grunted, and then he thrust hard one last time, and straightened and stilled as his release pumped into me. His head fell forward and he stayed like that for a moment, spent.

We eventually pulled apart and he let me down to stand next to him.

J smoothed my hair so it hooked behind my ear and then he kissed me, a slow and lazy kiss and I could feel the smile forming on his lips. "So fucking good, baby," he murmured as he ended the kiss.

I laid my palm across his cheek. "I'm sorry I overreacted," I apologised, my head so much clearer.

His face lit up in a wicked grin. "Yeah, me too, but only a little bit because it meant I got to fuck you like that."

"You can fuck me like that anytime you want. In fact, if you don't, I might just unleash my inner bitch on you so that you do," I promised.

He grinned at me for a moment longer and then said, "Okay, time to get you clean and then to sleep."

FIFTEEN MINUTES later we were in bed, me on my side and J behind me with his arms and legs wrapped around and over me. He murmured in my ear, "Goodnight, beautiful. I love you."

Yep, this and J were home. "I love you, too," I replied and drifted off to sleep.

15

JASON

WEDNESDAY ROLLED AROUND and it was back to club business. With Nix out of the picture, we could focus solely on our business interests and I sensed a distinct change in attitude in the clubhouse that morning. Marcus had called a meeting for ten a.m. and he outlined where we were at with key dealings. Storm had numerous business interests – restaurants, retail outlets, clubs – all legit, because we liked to keep our nose clean these days. We moved ourselves out of drugs years earlier and it had taken a lot of heat off the club. Currently, we had some distribution problems that needed resolving and he asked Scott and me to deal with that while he handed other jobs off to everyone else. The meeting was finished by ten thirty, and I was about to head out with Scott when Marcus stopped me.

"I had a talk with Madison last night. Seems she thinks she's gonna be okay. I'm not convinced and need to know where you think her head is at," he said.

"She told you we're back together?" I asked.

He shook his head. "No, but any fool could work that out, J. And to be honest, I think that's a good fuckin' thing. She needs someone like you to pull her into line and I'm hopin' like hell that you can help her keep her shit together. All this stuff with Nix and Bec must be doin' her head in, but she's fuckin' stubborn and won't talk about it." He was frustrated and with good reason; Madison could be a pain in the ass when it came to leaning on others for support.

"I think she's stronger than you give her credit for. Your daughter's a fighter, Marcus, and yeah, she doesn't like to talk about shit, but she's obviously learnt other ways of dealing with it. I'm keeping an eye on her and will let you know if anything comes up," I replied.

Marcus's steady gaze lingered on me for another moment, taking in everything I had said and then he nodded, "Okay. Good. I'll leave that with you." He seemed reassured and I left him to find Scott so we could go and sort out this distribution issue.

∾

"So, you and Madison, huh?" Scott looked over at me as we drove back to the clubhouse. We had been out all day dealing with problems and I was more than ready to call it a day. Madison called around lunch time to tell me she was going out job hunting and to organise to meet me at the clubhouse by five o'clock. It was nearly five now and I was distracted thinking about her. "Brother, did you hear me?" Scott pulled me from my thoughts.

"Yeah, we're together," I confirmed.

"Good, it's about fuckin' time."

I chuckled. "Seems you and Marcus can agree on that. It's a work in progress but mark it, I'm gonna marry her one day."

Scott snapped his head in my direction, a stunned look on his face. "Yeah?"

"Yeah. Haven't told her yet though," I answered.

Scott laughed. "Uh, I hate to break it to you, but you don't generally tell a woman you're gonna marry her, J. And I really hate to fuckin' break this bit of news to you, but nobody tells Madison to do anything."

"Mark my words, brother. I might ask her, I might tell her, but either way, it's happening."

"You two are made for each other, both as stubborn as fuck." He shook his head.

As we pulled into the parking lot of the clubhouse, Madison was walking towards the front door and I took in her sexy dress and heels. Her long hair was up in a ponytail, which excited my dick. Christ, I couldn't wait to get her upstairs. She turned and waved at me before going inside.

Scott looked at me, shaking his head. "Keep your dick in your pants."

"You wait till you find someone, Scott, and then you'll understand."

"Not fuckin' likely," he muttered.

I found her sitting at the bar with Stoney. I liked Stoney, but I didn't like the way he was looking at Madison. "Eyes off her tits, Stoney," I snapped.

Madison's eyes widened and I waited for her response but she surprised the fuck out of me with her silence.

"Yeah, yeah," he grumbled, moving off his stool to stand. "I'm outta here."

"His eyes weren't on my tits, J," she said as we watched him leave.

"Yeah, baby, they were."

She rolled her eyes. "You weren't even standing in front of him to be able to know that."

I moved into her space, pushed my body up against her side and wrapped one arm around her shoulders. We were now the only ones in the bar. Leaning my face down, I spoke into her ear, "I know they were because you're wearing a low cut, tight dress that your tits are almost spilling out of, and it's exactly where my eyes would have been if I was Stoney."

Madison's lips parted and her tongue darted out to touch them. My eyes took in the rapid rising and falling of her chest; I knew that she was wet and I pushed my erection harder into her side before stepping away slightly. She stood swiftly and turned to press her body into mine, reaching her hand down to rub my dick. I groaned and put my arms around her, gripping her ponytail and pulling her head backwards. Dipping my head, I licked up her throat and then took her mouth in a hard kiss. She was like a wild fucking animal, kissing and tonguing me, all the while rubbing up and down my dick with one hand, the other on my ass.

I abruptly ended the kiss and she whimpered, clearly not ready to let go. "I'm gonna come in my pants if we don't stop," I muttered.

"Fucking tease," she complained. "I'm so wet for you right now, J. You don't know what you're missing." Her hands stopped what they were doing and she pushed me away. Fuck, she was glorious; her face was flushed, lips swollen, nipples hard and it took all my control not to throw her over my shoulder and continue this upstairs.

"We need to talk," I said, and with those four words, I killed the mood completely.

Madison's body tensed. "About?"

I sighed and reached for her arm. "Not here, babe. In my room," I said, and guided her out of the bar, towards the stairs.

We walked in silence, and when we reached my door, she turned to me and asked, "Am I going to like this talk, J? Because I've had a really good day and I don't want to ruin it."

I ignored her question and ushered her inside. "Sit on the couch, baby, and no, you probably won't like this talk, but we need to have it, and once it's done, I promise it will be the last time we discuss it."

I expected an argument but she surprised me for the second time that day by doing as I said, sitting and waiting patiently for me to start talking.

Moving to sit next to her, I took a minute to get the words out because I needed to say this right. "For us to move forward, we need to sort out the shit we left behind last time; the shit we didn't sort out then," I asserted, and let her take that in before continuing, "What happened with Rob really screwed us and I'm still not sure why, but I know that was when it all started to fall apart. I need you to tell me why."

A pained look crossed her face and she sat right back in the couch, away from me. I reached out to hold her hand, but she snatched it away, placing it over the scar on her arm instead. Taking a deep breath she began, "Growing up, my dad sheltered me from the club a lot. Sure, I knew the guys and they were my family, but I didn't know about the guns, the drugs or the violence. You know that already. When I started seeing it, I wasn't concerned by it, or so I thought…" she stopped for a moment, getting herself together, "…until that night, J. When I saw what you were capable of and what Scott was capable of, it freaked me the fuck out. Neither of you seemed fazed by what you did, and at the time, it bothered me. I didn't know how to deal with it. I also felt guilty that it was all my fault."

"Rob was trying to rape you, Madison. He sliced your fucking arm and attacked you, and I couldn't stop him so I did what I had to do," I pointed out calmly.

"I get that, but the way you two just dealt with his body and carried on like nothing had happened… I found that hard to comprehend." She was honest, and even though I didn't like what she was saying, I was relieved that she was finally being open with me.

"Do you think that I like that part of me? That I enjoy doing the dirty work that being in the club requires? I fucking don't. But I do it for a reason. And six years ago, when I fell in love with you, my reason became you."

Her eyes widened, and for a moment she just stared at me. I had no idea what she was thinking until she finally said, "I know. I realise that now, J, but I didn't back then. I didn't work that out until I talked to Mum yesterday. I get it, and I'm okay with it."

I cocked my head. "Really, baby? How can you go from not sure to totally okay in a day?"

She smiled and it hit my heart; it was so pure and genuine. Then she moved back towards me on the couch and touched my chest, and that fucking hit my dick. God, this woman turned me the fuck on. "J, we went through so much, and I let it break me, but having to put myself back together has made me strong, stronger than I've ever been. I didn't get this until now. I also didn't get just what we had, how we fit together. I didn't appreciate you and what you are willing to do for me. Mum helped me see that, and she made me realise I need to trust you more. I don't know if I'll ever be totally okay with all the stuff you have to do for the club, but I'm okay with putting my trust in you and in the fact that you do it for me and our families."

Fuck. Mind blown. I hadn't realised she had come this far. "To give me that is to give me everything," I confessed.

Nodding, she said, "I thought I had given you all I had to give, but this is the final piece of me. Now you have it all."

Fuck. "Thank you, baby." I leaned forward to catch her lips in a kiss.

She kissed me, but then pulled away with a sly grin. "Don't think this means I will roll over and let you control me though."

I chuckled. "Wouldn't dream of it, baby. You wouldn't be you without that fucking attitude and that need to argue with every damn thing I say."

"Good. Now, are you going to fuck me?" she demanded, reaching her hand to touch my dick.

16

MADISON

J SAT ON the edge of the bed, putting his boots on, but also watching me get dressed. The desire in his eyes was clear, and even though we had just had mind blowing sex, both of us wanted more. However, we had agreed to go to dinner at Mum and Dad's.

"Why did you say yes to dinner? I could have fucked you all night, baby," he grumbled, finishing with his boots and standing.

I smoothed my dress down and slipped on my heels, noting J's eyes slide down my legs and then back up to my breasts as I adjusted the top. Fuck, I loved it when he watched me with such intensity.

He took a determined step towards me and snaked his arms around my waist, letting his hands drop to my ass. On contact, I grew wet again as his hard cock rubbed up against my body. I hadn't bothered answering him, and he breathed into my ear, "Dinner will be quick because I need to get my cock back in you real fucking soon."

Fuck. White hot desire coursed through me. My hands rested on his chest and I wound one up past his neck to tangle my fingers in his hair and pulled his lips down to mine. He willingly took my mouth, and our lips and tongues came together in a frenzy of love and lust.

J ended the kiss and separated us. "Jesus, Madison, I can't get enough of you."

I smiled. "Good, baby, and you better feel that way for the rest of your life."

"With that pussy and those tits and legs, I have no doubt," he said, and then, "Now, let's get going because the sooner we get there, the sooner I can get you out of there."

On the drive over, he asked, "So, what did you get up to today?"

Warmth hit me. It was always the simple things like this that made me the happiest. Being with J, talking about our day, driving to dinner together; these were the things that brought a smile to my face and filled my heart with joy. "I visited your sister and Crystal this morning and then I went job hunting this afternoon."

He raised his eyebrows. "You visited Brooke? How the fuck did that go?"

I laughed. "Actually, it went really well. We had a good talk about things and cleared the air. She was supportive of us and I think she genuinely meant it. She's different, J."

"Yeah, losing Bec has hit her hard and I think she's

done a lot of thinking since it happened."

"Well, we've put the past behind us, and I'm happy about that because it will make it easier for you and me, and also for me to help out with Crystal."

He nodded in agreement. "Speaking of Bec, the club is organising her and Georgie's funeral for Friday morning."

"Okay, I'll let Brooke know so we can prepare Crystal for it," I said, dreading the day, and that an innocent child had to even go through this shit.

"Good. Now, tell me about your job hunting," he said, moving onto a much better topic of conversation.

I smiled broadly. "I got a job! I'll be starting next week at that little clothing boutique on East Street."

"That's great, baby. Sounds like you had a really good day," he said, draping his arm across the back of my seat, his eyes sweeping down my body and back to my eyes before fixing a lazy grin on me.

My heart fluttered. This was happiness to me and I was so glad to have another chance at it with J.

DINNER with my parents started out as a standard affair. Mum was her usual self, fussing over everybody, making sure we were well fed and trying to stick her nose in everyone's business. Dad was in a pensive mood and was fairly quiet throughout the night. J was his cocky self, doing all he could to hurry it along so he could get us home and satisfy his desire for me.

And then my mother asked me a question that changed

the mood of the night. "So, honey, have you decided if you will move in here with us until you get yourself sorted out?"

J's head snapped up. "No, she's moving in with me," he said.

Mum didn't miss a beat. "Don't you two want some time to settle back into your relationship before moving in together again?" She was staring straight at J, not even glancing in my direction. I didn't know what was going on here, but it felt like some secret communication was taking place.

J scowled at her. "No, Sharon, we don't want some time. We've wasted enough time already."

Normally, I would be jumping right in here to tell J to let me make my own damn decisions, but I wanted to see how this played out between him and mum.

"Has Madison agreed to this J, or are you back to making all the decisions in your relationship?" Shit, Mum was stepping into unsafe territory.

J's nostrils flared, and he was about to say something when my father spoke, "That's enough, Sharon. This is between J and Madison. It has nothing to do with us."

My mother's head spun to face my father and she snapped at him, "Well, it will have something to do with us if Madison isn't ready for it yet. I worry what will happen if she can't handle it again."

Oh, fuck me! They were talking about my drinking, and it pissed me off that none of them could just come out and say that to start with. I slammed my chair back and stood. "Just an FYI for you all, you know, because you never actually asked me, my drinking is under control. I haven't touched a drop of alcohol in nearly two fucking years. Mum, I am moving in with J,"—I fixed my glare on him—"Even though he never took the time to ask me. I do appreciate the concern, but I'm working through stuff in my head, and I think I'm going to be okay. I think I'm finally getting my shit together."

J's anger had dissipated and he was calm as he said to my mother, "We're working it out together, and no, I'm not making all the decisions. I know I'm a bossy asshole but I'll do anything to make this work."

Mum appraised him and then nodded, "I hope so, J, for both your sakes. I love you like a son, and when I say I'm worried, it's not just for Madison. I saw what you went through last time too."

I sat back down and put my hand on J's arm, gently rubbing it. We held each other's gaze for a moment and then I turned to look at Mum. "Thanks, Mum. It means a lot to me that you feel that way about J." J just grunted in response; if it had been anyone other than my mother bringing this up, he would have told them to fuck off and mind their own business. I loved that, for me, he showed her respect and answered her questions.

We were all saved from this conversation when Dad's phone rang. He stood and took the call in another room and Mum started clearing the table.

I murmured to J, "You *are* a bossy motherfucker. When were you going to have that discussion with me? The one about me moving in?"

He grinned. "I wasn't, babe. It was a fucking given."

I rolled my eyes. "Of course it was."

Dad came back, hard eyes fixed on J. "You and me. Now." He indicated with his head that they were to leave and J was straight up, concern visible on his face.

He leant down, took my face with both his hands and kissed my forehead. "You stay with your mum till we're back."

I fought the need to ask what was going on and simply nodded in agreement. "Okay, baby," I replied.

Mum and I watched in silence as they left, neither of us sure what was happening, both of us being guided by faith and trust. I had come a long way in the last few days.

*J*ASON

M*ARCUS* and I entered the bar, scanning the room for Scott. He was keeping an eye out and saw us straight away. Seated next to him was Nash, and across from them were Bullet and one of his boys. They made room for us to sit as we approached; I was nervous about what this meeting meant and sat with some trepidation.

Marcus spoke first, "What the fuck's so important to drag me away from a family dinner?" He glared at Bullet; there wasn't much love lost between these two. They had come to blows over club dealings in the past and Marcus didn't trust him at all.

Bullet's jaw clenched. "Got word that Nix's crazy sister is out for blood. Thought you should know."

"What are we talking here?" Marcus asked.

"She's threatened your family, Madison especially."

"Fuck!" I roared and slammed my hand down on the table. "When the fuck does all this shit end?"

Bullet threw his hands up in a defensive stance. "Got nothing to do with me. I'm just showing some courtesy by letting you know what I've heard. I figure it's the least I can do after what Nix put your club through."

Scott leaned forward, a menacing tone to his voice, "Where the fuck is this bitch?"

"We've lost her. After we heard she'd made threats, I sent some of the boys around to see her. Seems they scared her off and she's done a runner, but I've still got concerns she means business." He pulled a piece of paper from his pocket and slid it across the table to Marcus. "This is a list of places to try first. We'll be out of town on a run the next few days but when we get back, I'll contact you, see if you've located her. Trust me; I want this shit dealt with once and for all too." He pushed his chair back and stood to leave.

"Once this is dealt with, we need a sit down. Nix fucked our club's relations and I want us to fix that, Bullet," Marcus said.

Bullet stopped mid-stride, and contemplated Marcus for a moment before replying, "Yeah, seems he did."

After they left, I looked at Marcus and ranted, "This is fucked up. I want to find that bitch and deal with her. No fucking loose ends this time, no fucking holding back."

"We find her first and see what she's playing at, J. No need to start a war where one's not needed," Marcus countered, and then continued, "Tomorrow, first thing, you, Scott and Nash follow these leads up."

I nodded, but I had no fucking intention of leaving that bitch to carry out her vendetta. This time, I would make sure Madison was safe and do whatever the fuck it took to make that happen.

17

MADISON

THE NEXT MORNING I woke at seven, alone in J's bed. He and Dad had come back from meeting with Bullet and told us about Nix's sister, Mandy. J appeared quite pissed off about it all, but Dad was pretty calm so I wasn't going to worry about it too much at this point. Although, I had met Mandy once and she was a crazy bitch, so perhaps I should be worried about it. J was going out with Scott and Nash to find her, but I hadn't expected him to leave so early, or without waking me first.

I got up, made coffee and then tried to phone J. My call went straight to message bank so I left him a message to call me back. Fifteen minutes later, he still hadn't called so I tried him again. Now I was beginning to feel like a nagging wife but I just wanted to say good morning. The call went to message bank again, so I left another message.

I hung up and put my phone down. That was it; no more calls to him until he rang me back.

It was time to get ready for the day. I had a yoga class booked for eight o'clock and then a hair appointment at one. After finishing my coffee, I had a shower, got dressed and was out the door. J had left me the keys to his Jeep, which I was grateful for. I arrived at the yoga studio ten minutes later and checked my phone; still nothing from J. It was starting to piss me off, but I tried to remind myself that he was technically at work so perhaps he was occupied with stuff. I shoved my phone in my bag and headed inside; I was more than ready for a session and hopefully the knot of tension I felt in my gut at the moment would be eased by the yoga.

JUST OVER AN HOUR later I was fumbling with the car keys trying to get them in the lock when my phone rang. Yoga hadn't smoothed any of the tension from my body, and as I struggled with everything in my arms in order to get to my phone, I threw a hissy fit and just let everything fall to the ground.

"Fuck!" I yelled as I retrieved the phone from the ground and answered it.

"Madison,"—it was Scott—"where the fuck is J?"

Well, fuck me. The day was quickly turning into one big 'ole pile of shit. Yes, where the fuck was J, if not with Scott? "I've got no idea," I snapped back at him. "I thought he was with you."

Scott was fuming. "Well, he should be, but he's not fuckin' here."

"I've left him two messages, but he hasn't replied to either of them."

"Yeah, not answering my calls either. Okay, gotta go," he said and hung up.

I was left staring at my phone. God, I loved the way my brother spoke to me. *Not.* And again, my mind swung to J. Where was he? I dialled him again, hoping he might actually answer my call this time. No fucking luck; it went to message bank yet again, and now I was really shitty. I picked up the rest of my crap that was strewn across the ground and finally unlocked the car door. Throwing everything on the passenger seat, I got in, started the car and threw it into reverse. Screaming out of the parking lot, I shoved my sunglasses on and turned the music up really fucking loud. What better way to drown in one's own shitty mood than with some Avenged Sevenfold.

I swung past his house hoping he might be there, but he wasn't, so I continued onto the clubhouse. As I parked the car, I saw Scott walking out the front door and quickly got out of the car to catch him before he left.

It had been about twenty minutes since I had spoken to him and he was still pissed off so I guessed that he hadn't found J yet.

"Any luck finding him?" I asked, as he approached me.

"Haven't spoken to him yet, but got word as to where he might be so we're heading out there now," he answered me gruffly.

"What's going on? Why has J gone off the grid today?"

I asked Scott, even though it was highly unlikely he would give me an answer. *A girl can try though, right?*

"Madison, I don't have time for twenty fuckin' questions right now," he barked.

I threw my hands up. "Fine! But when you find him, tell him I expect a call."

Scott shook his head, clearly exasperated. "I'm not getting involved in your drama with J. That shit's between the two of you."

He walked past me towards his bike and I flipped him the bird. Even though he didn't see it, it still made me feel good. "Fuck you, too!" I yelled and stormed off in the direction of the clubhouse.

A few minutes later, the rumble of bikes sounded as he and a couple of the boys left. Pissed at both J and Scott, I needed to vent so I pulled out my phone as I headed inside. Dialling Serena, I noted how empty the clubhouse was and thanked the universe for some peace and quiet.

Serena answered on the first ring. "Why haven't I heard from you for days?"

I laughed. "Well, why haven't I heard from you? And it hasn't been days, you drama queen!"

"I've been busy screwing hot guys. What's your excuse, chica?"

"Oh, I bet you have." I had no doubt that was exactly what she had been doing. "I've been busy screwing one hot guy," I answered her with a wicked grin on my face.

She squealed. "Tell me it's J!"

"Of course it's J," I chastised her.

"It's about time you two did the dirty," she teased, and

I could hear the approval in her voice. "So, how is the moody motherfucker?"

I groaned. "I couldn't tell you how he is today because the asshole left before I woke up and hasn't returned any of my calls."

"Oh...trouble in paradise so soon. Doesn't sound good," she said.

"Well, I have some other news for you. Nix is dead. Don't ask, it's a long story. But, his sister has made threats against us, so I think J is busy looking into that. Still...he should call me back, so I'm annoyed at him."

"Perhaps you should withhold the love tonight, babe," she joked.

I laughed. "You always know how to cheer me up, honey. Thank you."

"Well, that's what best friends are for. I think I need to come for a visit. How about this weekend?"

"Yes! Do you think Gina would give you Friday or Monday off as well so you could stay for longer?" I asked, excited at the thought of seeing her. It had only been a few days since I'd left but I really missed her.

"I'll ask and will let you know," she promised.

We chatted for a couple more minutes and then hung up. I felt so much better after talking with her; I had known she would lift me out of the shitty mood I was in. I sat quietly for a moment, thinking about our friendship and what it meant to me; how it had helped me through a really tough part of my life. I wasn't sure how I would have gotten through all of that without her, and I smiled thinking about it, and also about how far I had come on my journey to give up alcohol.

"What's got you smilin' like a bitch who just had good cock?" I was interrupted by a sexy drawl.

I looked up to see Nash leaning against the door frame, arms crossed in front of him, sexy smirk plastered on his face. He was tall, all muscle and ink; he exuded a couldn't-give-a-fuck attitude. Nash was one of the cockiest men I had ever met and the women flocked to him.

I rolled my eyes. "Can a woman not smile unless she's had cock?" I asked.

He uncrossed his arms and pushed away from the door frame coming towards me. "No, sweet thing, it all comes down to cock."

"Well, I hate to tell you, Nash, but this woman hasn't had any today, and yet I'm still smiling. I think your theory is a little off." I loved bantering back and forth with him.

He raised his eyebrows. "J's fallin' down on the job there, sweetheart. You sure you don't want to jump ships? I've got all you'll ever need." He grinned at me, opening his arms wide in an inviting gesture.

"You never give up, do you?"

He shook his head. "Not where you're concerned. Until J makes an old lady out of you, I figure I've still got a shot."

"Sorry to burst your bubble but I really am taken, and as much as he pisses me off at times, I think it's a forever thing."

He cocked his head to the side and contemplated me for a moment. "You're serious there, aren't you?"

"Yeah, Nash, I am," I replied.

The flirty tone of the conversation had just been replaced, and Nash pulled up a stool. "So, what's givin' you that smile today, if it's not J?" he asked, genuine interest on his face.

I wasn't one to share thoughts and feelings very often, and although we shared a flirty friendship, I had never really had a deep conversation with Nash. But something compelled me to open up to him. "I was just thinking about my friendship with my best friend, and also about how I've given up drinking. That was fucking hard to do, Nash, but I hardly think about having a drink these days."

"That's fuckin' great, sweetheart. And I should know because I have been where you are, and I know how hard it is to kick that addiction." He surprised me because I didn't know he was an alcoholic.

I leaned closer to him, almost like we were sharing secrets that no one else could know about. "You're an alcoholic?"

"It's been just over five years since I've had a drink, but I still have my days where I want one. I remember how you were before you left and you've come a long fuckin' way. Best thing you ever did, getting outta here then. You reckon you can handle being back? Being with J? 'Cause being an old lady isn't a piece of fuckin' cake, sweetheart," he said.

"Honestly? I'm going to give it a good go but I hear you. I know being with J won't be easy, but I've realised things about him and the club that make me think it will be different this time. I'll be different in the way I react to stuff."

He leaned even closer to me and grazed my cheek with his thumb, his minty breath in the air between us. "You're a strong woman, Madison, and J is a fuckin' lucky man to have you. If you ever need someone to talk to, someone who understands how fuckin' hard it is to battle this shit, you just call me. Okay?"

I nodded, overcome by emotion. Having never seen this side of Nash, I was surprised into silence for a moment. He pulled his hand away and leaned back on his stool, serious for another few moments, and then he flashed me that sexy grin of his. "Okay, sweetheart, I'll leave you to it. Gotta get back to work or your daddy will have my balls," he said.

"Thanks, Nash," I said, quietly. "That means a lot to me."

He winked at me. "Of course, if you ever get sick of J not sharin' his dick with you, I can take care of that too." And he was back to his cocky self.

I smacked his ass as he walked away which really only encouraged him, and I rolled my eyes again as he looked back at me to blow me an air kiss. Laughing, he finally left the room and I was still smiling like an idiot ten minutes later when Scott and J found me.

They stormed into the club bar where I was sitting, yelling at each other, not realising that I was in there.

"I don't give a fuck what you or Marcus say about it. This time I am not leaving loose ends, Scott. This time I am going to do what I should have done last fucking time," J roared, eyes blazing, body tense. He even scared me a little when he was like this.

"No! You need to calm the fuck down and get your head straight, brother. You do this, and there's no telling where this shit will end. That chick has connections, and you piss those connections off, you could be bringing hurt to the club, the likes we haven't ever seen," Scott yelled back, trying to talk some sense into him, but I could see that J was focused on his own agenda.

"Fuck her, and fuck her connections! Madison needs —" and at that point, J saw me and stopped dead in his tracks. He took a moment and then started yelling at me, "What the fuck, Madison? Why are you here?"

"I was looking for you." I stood then walked to him. Jabbing my finger at his chest, I continued, "God, you can be an asshole sometimes. You left before I woke up this morning and haven't returned any of my calls, and now you speak to me like that." I shook my head at him. "Not happening, J. Come and find me when you're ready to apologise." We glared at each other while that sunk in, and then I turned, grabbed my bag and headed outside. I expected him to follow me out, but he didn't and that pissed me off even more. Fuck, could this day get any worse?

SEVEN HOURS LATER, I was thinking that yes, the day could in fact get worse. Having left the hairdressers, I walked to the car and saw J leaning against it. He hadn't bothered to call me, and I had stewed on that all afternoon. As a result, I was in the kind of mood where I could reach out, grab his balls, and yank them the fuck off. With one fucking hand. While punching him in the face with my other hand.

As I approached, he stayed where he was; shades in place, arms crossed and looking sexy as fuck. But I wasn't getting sucked in by that. I had balls to rip off, so I stalked up to him and snapped, "Seven fucking hours, J! I thought we were doing it differently this time."

"I had things to take care of," he growled, still not moving from where he was.

"Things that were more important than me?" I was possibly being a bit selfish here but fuck it. I needed him to step up and put me first.

He ripped his shades off, his eyes dark and flinty. "Yeah, babe. Things that were more important than you, and let's get this straight from the get go, I'm not at your fucking beck and call. That's not me and you know that, so don't start trying to change that, 'cause it ain't happening."

"I don't want you at my beck and call. I just wanted a damn apology!" I yelled.

"What the fuck for?"

"Seriously? We've got a lot of work ahead of us, J, if you need to ask me that." I gestured with my hands for him to move out of the way so that I could get in the car.

He shook his head. "Passenger side, babe,"—he held up a set of keys—"I'm driving."

I looked around for his bike but couldn't see it. Scowling, I muttered, "Oh, fuck me." Knowing there was no point arguing with him, I did as he said.

"You didn't answer me. What am I supposed to be apologising for?" he asked as he settled into the driver's seat, eyes focused on me, a hint of anger still there.

"I did answer you. As far as I'm concerned, you need to work that out for yourself." Why did men always need things spelled out for them?

"Madison, it would be a lot fucking quicker for you to just tell me."

"And I'd be a lot fucking happier if I didn't have to tell you." I blew out an angry breath, "Just take me home, J. I don't want to talk about this anymore." I turned away from him and stared out the front of the car, willing him not to say another word because, if he did, I might just reach over and do some damage that both of us would regret.

We sat in a heated silence for awhile until, finally, he started the car and took us home, the day having gone to complete shit.

18

JASON

I SAT ON the couch, mindlessly flicking through channels on the television. It was nearly midnight, and Madison and I still hadn't spoken since we arrived home that afternoon. She secluded herself in the bedroom as soon as we got home and hadn't come out since. It pissed me off at the time, but in hindsight, it was probably the smartest move she could've made. After a long, stressful day that achieved fucking nothing, I had been all out of patience and she had fucking tested me.

Wanting to catch up with Nix's sister, Mandy, I had headed out early to find her. I doubted that Marcus and Scott would deal with her once and for all, not wanting to stir up trouble, so it was up to me to make sure she didn't fuck with Madison. All day I had chased the bitch with nothing to show for it. She was gone, and no one seemed to know where she was. On top of that, I had Scott breathing down my neck and Madison yelling at me for God only knew what. Fuck, I was beginning to think she would be the death of me. And yet, all I wanted to do was get my dick into her sweet pussy.

Christ, I was getting hard thinking about it. I undid my jeans and reached in, wrapping my hand around my dick. Shutting my eyes, I pictured Madison's hand around it and her lips on me. Fuck, the imagery was too much; I needed her actual hands and lips. I got up and stalked into the bedroom. She was lying on her side and rolled onto her back at the sound of me entering the room. Her long hair was splayed across the bed, and all she had on were her panties and a thin t-shirt that clearly showed her hard nipples.

I lifted my shirt over my head and discarded it, along with my jeans while she watched, her hands moving to her tits. My breathing became erratic and I could smell the desire swirling around us. I indicated with my finger that she should take her clothes off and grunted, "Off, and then show me how you want me to touch you, baby."

She sat up and removed her top, eyes on mine before they dropped to my dick. Entranced with what she saw there, she lay back and slowly peeled her panties down, not moving her gaze from my dick. Lifting two fingers to her mouth she sucked them and then moved them to her pussy, swirling around her clit while her other hand tweaked one of her nipples. Satisfaction shot through her because she moaned loudly, and then lifted her ass slightly off the bed before pushing both fingers inside her wet pussy. Her other hand moved down to stroke her clit, and she closed her eyes as she worked towards an orgasm.

I liked to watch but the need to taste her, to have her, took over and I positioned myself on the bed with my head between her legs and my hands on either side of her. Her eyes flew open and she shot me a sexy smile before tangling both her hands in my hair and pushing my face down into her pussy. I inhaled the smell I loved so much and ran my tongue from one end to the other before dipping it inside and tasting her sweet juices. Fuck, she was wet and it got me even harder. I moved one hand down to my dick to give it a hard couple of tugs while I continued to tongue her. Getting carried away, I kept pumping until suddenly, I needed to be inside her. Moving quickly, I knelt, spread her legs wide and pulled her to me so that my dick was at her entrance. My eyes roamed over her body, taking in her glorious fucking tits, and then they found her eyes, locked on mine and full of desire.

"Fuck, baby. I've gotta have you," I managed to get out before she tugged me to her, pulling my dick into her.

I entered her, thrusting hard and fast. Her walls clamped around me and it did fucking beautiful things to me. Madison was a greedy bitch with a greedy pussy, and fucking her was an out-of-this-world experience. I continued to thrust in and out while leaning down to kiss her. Her legs were around me, and her hands grabbed my face and she kissed me back, hard and hungry. We kept at this for awhile and then she pulled away from my kiss.

"Top, J. I want to be on top," she grunted, and I flipped us so that she was on top, straddling me.

I let her take control, and exhaled in pleasure as she wiggled backwards and leant down, taking my dick in her mouth. She sucked me hard and reached her hand to massage my balls. Coming up for air, she murmured, "Love your cock, honey. Love sucking it, but I fucking need it in me."

I wanted that too, but I wanted to watch her for a bit longer. "Not yet, babe. I want to watch you some more. Want to watch your finger in your pussy while your other hand is wrapped around my cock."

Her eyes lit up at this; yeah she fucking loved me watching her just as much as I loved watching her. She moved so her chest was on mine, legs still straddling me and ground her pussy against my dick while she licked my lips and kissed me, slowly, lazily. I wrapped my arms around her, letting my hand slide over her ass, and then dipped a finger into her pussy from behind, pushing slowly, in and out. I could feel her lips curling into a smile while I kissed her and she moaned against my lips, "Feels so good, baby. My turn now."

I stopped what I was doing and she moved back to a sitting position, legs on either side of me. She spread her legs and tilted her pussy forward. With our eyes locked, she started stroking herself. I shifted my gaze to take it all in, waiting patiently for her to take hold of my cock. I was so fucking hard, and watching her pleasure herself only intensified it. She continued to stroke and finger herself and I started to grow impatient; I needed her hands on my dick.

"Babe. Dick," I ordered, and she grinned wickedly at me, the fucking tease. She knew exactly what she was doing to me.

When her hand grasped my cock a moment later, pleasure shot through me and I shut my eyes for a moment before opening them again and focusing my gaze on what her hands were doing. One hand was fingering herself and the other was pumping my cock; it was fucking heaven, and I felt it build in me. She was getting closer too. Her eyes were at half-mast and she bit her bottom lip while her tongue darted out every now and then to lick them.

Just as I was about to tell her to get her sweet pussy onto my dick, she stopped everything she was doing, and did just as I wanted. I groaned as she sank down onto me and when she started moving, I reached my hands to grip onto her ass. The pressure built and she fucked me harder, tits bouncing all over the place, and I enjoyed the view; it was a fucking glorious sight. And then she screamed as the orgasm hit her. Throwing her head back, she closed her eyes as she let it take over her body. I reached my hands around to her tits and started pumping my dick up into her, trying to find my own release. And it was so fucking close; I could feel it coming as I pumped, and pumped, and then it hit. *Fuck me! Fucking hell!* I came hard, and we held onto it for as long as we could.

Coming off the high, she lay down next to me on her back, one hand flung across my stomach. I placed my hand over hers, lacing our fingers together, and waited to see if she was still angry at me. Madison was highly unpredictable. Well, as far as I was concerned, she was. Make-up sex seemed to calm her, so I could only fucking hope.

She turned to look at me, so I rolled onto my side, propping my body up on my elbow. Tracing a line on her stomach, I started, "I'm sorry, babe."

"Do you even know what you are sorry for, J?" she

asked, with that slightly frustrated tone that she often took with me.

"For a million fucking things, but mostly for being an asshole to you today, and for not returning your calls," I answered her truthfully.

Her eyes searched mine for a moment and then she said, "You *were* an asshole to me today and I didn't like it. I get that you were busy with work but you've got to understand that I was worried about you. With all the shit going on at the moment, I needed to hear your voice, needed to know you were okay. And then to speak to me the way you did… that hurt, J." Her vulnerability shone through her voice, hitting me square in the chest.

I reached my hand up to her face and cupped her cheek. "This is gonna take a lot of work, isn't it?"

Confusion flashed across her face. "Do you want out?" she half whispered, and I could sense the tension settling over her.

"No, baby. I told you this was forever, and I meant it. It's just hitting me now, though, how much we are going to have to put in to make it good. But I need you to know that I want to do the work. I want this to be the best damn thing in our lives."

She took a moment to process my words and I knew when she had, because she let the tension in her body go and smiled. "Me too, J. I tried so hard today not to get mad at you about the phone calls and I'm sorry if it came across like I was trying to keep track of you, because I really wasn't. I don't expect you to be there whenever I want you, and I'm not trying to change you."

"Right. So, tomorrow we make it better. But, I need you to know that this could take some time on my end."

She laughed. "Yeah, baby, because changing assholey ways is a very time-consuming project. You're just lucky I'm a patient woman."

I grinned at her and thanked my lucky fucking stars for her. No other woman would ever come close to her.

19

Madison

FRIDAY FLEW BY, and before I knew it, it was the afternoon and I was waiting at the clubhouse for Serena to arrive. It had been a long and at times hard week, and I was so grateful she was coming to visit. The funeral for Bec and Georgie had been that morning, and it had been tough to sit through. Thinking about the lives needlessly taken, and watching Crystal deal with her loss, was awful. She was a strong girl, but I worried about her and probably always would. Brooke seemed to be coping well with Crystal, and I surprised myself, but I was happy they had each other.

After the funeral, J had to do some club work. When I asked him what it was, he got shitty with me and said I had to trust him, and stop asking those types of questions. This had, of course, led to an argument, because all I had been trying to do was show an interest in what he did. I apologised and tried to explain where I'd been coming from, but I'd already annoyed him and so we hadn't resolved it before he left.

I checked my watch. It was just after four o'clock and I still hadn't heard from Serena. Needing some fresh air, I took myself outside and sat on the hood of J's Jeep. Going over and over my conversation with him from that morning was not helping me; it was just making me frustrated with the whole situation. And that was not good for our relationship.

I heard the rumble of a bike, and turned to see J pulling in. He parked his bike and walked towards me, a grim look on his face. "Babe, what are you doing out here by yourself?" he asked, coming to a stop just in front of me, but making no move to kiss me hello.

I slid off the car to put myself closer to him, and put my hand on his chest; our bodies almost touching. "I've been thinking about stuff. About you."

He frowned. "What stuff?"

"I'm sorry I caused a misunderstanding between us this morning. I want to know about the things going on in your life, that's all. Not necessarily about your club stuff, just about *you*."

His body relaxed and he placed his hand over mine on his chest. Breathing out a long breath, he said, "Okay." He paused for a moment before adding, "Do you trust me? Trust that anything I do is done for a good reason?"

"I do, but—"

He cut me off. "Either you do, or you don't, babe."

"Okay, I do."

He nodded. "Right, so you need to trust me on this one."

We stood, eyeing each other while I weighed what he had said. Finally, I agreed, "All right, I will."

"Good," he muttered, and pulled me to him, wrapping me in his arms. He laid a kiss on the top of my head, and then said, "I love you. Love what you do for me."

"I love you, too." And I did. But fuck this was hard; fighting against all my instincts to need to know more. I just hoped that over time it would get easier, and that we would find a happy middle ground where he would share some things and I would be able to let some things go.

I HUNG UP FROM SERENA, disappointed. One of the girls she worked with had been in a car accident and was stuck in hospital, which meant that Serena had to cover all of her shifts. Although I was sorry for her workmate, it meant that I wouldn't get to see her anytime soon and that sucked. I'd been looking forward to girly time this weekend, especially some deep and meaningfuls about my relationship with J. Serena had a way of helping me see situations from a different angle, and I felt like I really needed her insights at the moment.

"What's got you all sad, sweet thing?"

I looked up to see Nash settling onto the stool next to me. We were sitting at the club bar which was starting to fill up. Friday nights were usually busy. I smiled at him and answered, "My best friend was supposed to be visiting for the weekend, but can't come now."

"Ah, I see. You wanna hang out with me instead?" He winked. "There's cock in it for you if you want."

I shoved him hard enough that he had to balance himself to stay on the stool, but we both laughed while I did it. "Oh, my God! You never stop, do you?" I said.

"What can I say… you inspire me." He grinned.

"Tell me, Nash, why don't you have a girlfriend? You're a good looking guy and you're fun, and I've seen the way the ladies are all over you."

He shrugged. "I don't need the hassle that would bring, sweetheart. Not when all I want is a bit of pussy, and like you said, that's easy enough to get whenever I want it."

"How old are you, Nash?"

"Thirty-five. Why?"

"Do you want kids? Maybe a wife one day?"

"Fuck, no!" He was emphatic.

I couldn't hide my surprise. "Really?"

"The world's got enough fucked-up people in it. I don't need to add to that, and as far as a wife goes, I don't want to be tied down to anything or anyone," he answered me, the joking tone of the conversation replaced with total seriousness.

I cocked my head. "But you're tied to Storm, aren't you?"

"Sure am, and that's the only family I'll ever be tied to," he said with absolute certainty.

I didn't get his decision, but there was no point pursuing it because who was I to tell him what to want, so I simply said, "Fair enough. It's your life."

He flashed his cheeky grin at me again, all seriousness gone. "You and J talking babies yet?"

I whacked him again. "God, no!"

He pretended to shield himself from me. "Settle down, darlin'. I'm just teasing you."

Of course, it was at this point when Nash and I were mucking about and smacking each other that J should walk into the room. I saw him stalking towards us. I took in the shitty look on his face, and instantly pulled away from Nash. It was an instinctual move; probably the right one given J's current mood.

"Nash," he growled when he got to us, "keep your fucking hands off Madison."

Nash stood up and stepped into J's space so they were head to head. His grin and laughing eyes had been replaced with a menacing glare as he said, "I didn't have my fuckin' hands on her."

Oh, God. That was my cue to leave these two alone. "I'll be back soon," I said, but neither of them really acknowledged me. Shaking my head, I walked in the direction of the ladies room, hoping that they sorted their issues out by the time I came back.

WHEN I RETURNED ten minutes later, Nash was gone and J was downing a beer. He didn't drink often so he must have had a bad day. As I reached him, I settled my hand on his lower back and asked, "Did you rip his head off?"

He turned to me, annoyance in his eyes. "I don't like the way he flirts with you."

"He's harmless and he knows where I stand."

"Well, I don't think he'll bother you again. I've sorted that out now," he grunted.

"Mmm, I'm sure you have," I mused.

"Did you get hold of Serena?" He changed the subject which was probably a good idea. We were in unsafe territory talking about Nash.

"Yeah, she's not coming. She can't get out of work."

"Sorry, babe. Looks like you're stuck with me for the weekend," he said, a wicked look crossing his face. "Can't be a bad thing. I'm sure we'll think of things to pass the time."

I moved closer to him and moved my hand down to his ass. "Promise?" I asked.

He leaned towards me and brushed my lips with his, grinning at me afterwards. "Absolutely. Now, let's get you home. I need to get inside you."

20

MADISON

I ROLLED OFF J, and laid on my back, arms sprawled and huge grin plastered on my face. "Fuck, anytime you want to do that again, just let me know."

He shifted onto his side so he was facing me and smiled. "I want to do that to you all the fucking time, baby."

I eyed him. "Well, you'll have to wait for a bit because we have shopping to do this morning."

He shook his head and looked pained. "You might have shopping to do, babe, but I sure as shit don't."

"Yes, you do. You're coming with me, to help me find new clothes," I informed him.

It was Saturday morning, and we had enjoyed a lazy sleep in and fantastic wake-up sex. It was time for J to man-up and come shopping with me.

"I think you can find clothes all by yourself," he

muttered as he got out of bed and walked towards the bathroom.

Just before he closed the door, I yelled out, "Yeah, you're right. I'll get some really short dresses and tight skirts."

He didn't reply but five minutes later when he emerged, he muttered, "Get up, babe. We've got shopping to do."

I smiled to myself. He was so easy to manipulate sometimes.

We got ready and were out the door an hour later, J grumbling that it had taken me so long to get ready. "I'm not sure why it takes you so long, babe."

I pointed at my face and my hair. "Do you think women just wake up looking this good?" I asked him.

"You looked good to me an hour ago, before you put all that shit on your face," he said, opening the car door for me and helping me in.

I smiled at him as he shut the door, and waited for him to come around the car and get in before saying, "Sometimes you say the sweetest things."

"So, how long does shopping take? Tell me it's quick," he almost begged.

I laughed. "You'll be home for dinner," I promised, with a teasing wink.

He rolled his eyes and muttered, "Fuck."

THREE HOURS LATER, I had purchased an entire new

wardrobe, and J had reached the end of his patience. I was surprised and impressed he had lasted that long. The morning had started out fun with him enjoying some private little shows as I tried on numerous outfits. This had almost ended in us screwing in one of the dressing rooms, but the sales assistant had put a stop to that and asked us to leave. J hadn't been impressed with her and had told her exactly what he thought of her, and her uptight pussy. She had threatened to call the police so I dragged him out of there before the situation got completely out of hand.

We had visited a stack of stores and J was insistent that this was the last one. I'd just tried on a dress I knew I had to have, and J was leaning against the changing room door watching me. Stepping out of the dress, I handed it to him and said, "This one's a definite."

He took it and eyed my body, clad only in bra and panties. "Babe, that's the last one. You're driving me crazy here. Three hours of watching you get in and out of dresses, and my dick is having a fit." He stepped closer to me and wrapped his hands around my ass, pulling me into him so that I could feel his erection. Dipping his head, he stole my mouth in a kiss. Hard and passionate, the kiss hit me in my core and I moaned with pleasure. He deepened the kiss, and reached one hand into my panties to touch my clit, slowly circling it. "You want me to fuck you with my finger or my dick?" His voice was low and rough.

"What do you think, baby?" I responded. As if there was any choice between the two.

He chuckled. "Thought so." Continuing to massage my clit, he backed me up against the wall, while I undid his jeans and pulled his cock free. I stroked it, circling the tip every couple of strokes. He groaned into my mouth, "Christ, babe. Really need in you now. This isn't gonna take long, not after you've been working me up all morning."

I lifted one leg to wrap around his waist and he pulled the other leg up. His cock sat at my entrance and, unable to wait any longer, I pushed myself against him so that he entered me. I was so wet for him that he slid straight in, filling me, and setting off a wave of pleasure.

J grunted as he pulled back out, and then thrust in hard, his balls slapping me. He set a fast pace and, knowing my tendency to scream, he lent his elbow against the wall to steady himself while he covered my mouth with his hand. It was a blur of bodies slapping together, eyes meeting between thrusts, and intense pleasure shooting through my body. J hadn't been kidding when he said it wouldn't last long; not even ten minutes later and he came, with me not far behind.

He leaned against me for a moment, and then pulled out and let me down. "That's what you get for teasing me for three fucking hours." He smirked, tucking his cock back into his jeans and fastening his jeans.

"I might bring you shopping more often, baby." I winked and got dressed.

Grabbing the dress I wanted to buy, J opened the door and we headed out to the sales counter to make our purchase. It was a busy Saturday morning in the shop, and from the looks we were getting, I was pretty sure everyone had heard us screwing. I just grinned at them, not giving a shit what anyone thought. The sales assistant fawned all over J as he paid for my dress. He hadn't let me pay for anything today, and after arguing with him for the first two hours, I had given up and just let him pay. Honestly, sometimes it was just easier not to argue with the man. And besides, I was grateful that he bought me all those clothes.

J finished up the transaction while I did my best to ignore the flirting that the sales assistant was doing. It really pissed me off though; she could see we were together, that he was buying me a dress and had most likely heard us having sex. So, why the fuck did she think it was okay to openly flirt with him in front of me?

I checked her name badge. Kate. Yeah, that figured. The only Kate's I knew were sluts, and this one wasn't any different.

"Fucking bitch," I grumbled under my breath, and J stopped what he was doing to turn and look at me.

He obviously hadn't heard what I said because he lent down and whispered in my ear, "What did you say, baby?"

As he pulled away to wait for my answer, I muttered, louder this time, "I said, fucking bitch."

He grinned at me, realising what I was getting at, and came back towards me, capturing my mouth in a passionate kiss. When he was finished, he said, "God, I love you."

I grinned back at him. "I love you too."

∾

J CONVINCED me to go on a bike ride with him that

afternoon. I figured it was only fair after he spent all morning shopping with me. Being on the back of his bike was something I enjoyed anyway, and it was a beautiful sunny day so I enjoyed the afternoon with him. We rode for just over an hour, heading out along the coastline. He bought us burgers and chips for lunch, and we sat on the beach and ate. I loved this quiet time with J, away from everyone else. Being back together meant that we had to figure each other out again. We had picked up almost like we had never been apart; we knew each other so well that it had been easy to do. However, as much as we knew each other, we had been apart for years and had both grown and changed a little, so I craved some time with him to discover these things about each other.

We arrived back home around five o'clock. Storm clouds had rolled in and the wind had picked up. Our plans for the night had been to go out for dinner and a movie, but with the change in the weather, we decided to order in and watch a movie at home. J had some calls to return before dinner so I jumped in the shower while he did that.

As I walked into the living room after my shower, I realised we had company. Scott was sitting with J on the couch, their heads together while they talked quietly. They stopped talking when they realised I had entered the room.

"Babe, I need to go out for awhile. There's been some trouble at Indigo that we need to sort out. Stoney's outside keeping watch until I get back," J said.

Indigo was one of the strip clubs that Storm owned, so I could only imagine the kind of trouble they had to go and sort out. I sighed. "Okay," I agreed, disappointed our evening had been wrecked.

They both stood and Scott headed outside, answering his ringing phone as he went. J came to me, and held my face with both his hands. He looked genuinely sorry, so I cut him some slack. "I'm sorry. I'll try and hurry things along so I can get back here soon," he promised, laying a quick kiss on my forehead.

And then he was gone. And I was alone on a Saturday night.

21

MADISON

J AND I settled into a routine over the next couple of months. Mandy no longer seemed to be a threat so life went on as normal. While still his usual bossy self, J backed off a little and gave me some space, which helped cement our relationship further. He dropped me off at work and picked me up when I was finished each day, while he took care of Storm business. Some days we also managed to get lunch together. Our nights were filled with time rebuilding our relationship. Some nights he got called out for club business, but thankfully, those nights weren't too often.

It was the weekends that I lived for. J was around for most of them, and along with spending time with our family and friends, we devoted a lot of time to just the two of us. When he said he would do the work to rebuild our relationship he'd been telling the truth, and I was the happiest I had ever been.

I was also trying hard to be a better girlfriend. This was hard sometimes, because J still refused to tell me much about club business. And it still pissed me off. Mostly though, I managed to keep my mouth shut and not argue with him about it. I was still hopeful that over time, he would come around.

Crystal was doing okay. J and I spent a lot of time with her and Brooke, and I was surprised at how well we were all getting along. We regularly helped Brooke out, looking after Crystal so she could have some time to herself. We were all still in shock that Bec was gone, and navigating our way through the grief tied us all together.

It was a Tuesday afternoon that my bubble burst. I was working at O's, the little boutique dress shop that I loved coming to every day, when a blast from my past waltzed in and blew shit all over my life.

"Mandy." I sucked in a breath, and fear sliced through me. The crazy look in her eyes scared the shit out of me, and my hand automatically reached for the phone to ring J.

As far as I knew, Mandy had disappeared and the club no longer considered her a threat. How wrong they had been about that.

"Don't!" she screamed. I dropped my hand. My heart rate picked up and my legs felt shaky. The room began to close in on me as I waited for her next move.

She stalked to where I was, not stopping until she was in my personal space. Her nostrils flared and I watched the veins popping in her neck. She jabbed a finger at my chest, the force making me momentarily lose my balance. "Nix's death is fucking on you, bitch! The day he met you, his death warrant was signed, and I'm going to fucking make you pay!" She screeched her warning.

Not often in life was i rendered speechless. It was, however, one of those times. My immediate reaction was to fight, but I quickly moved through scenarios of how that could play out, and decided against it. Assessing her, I thought she was probably high, and that was not a good thing to go up against. Thank goodness there were no customers or other staff in the store for her to threaten.

I didn't have to wait long to see what she would do next. She glared at me, daggers in her look, and then she shoved me backwards, and turned and strode to the door.

Before she closed the door, she shot one last threat at me, "You better watch your back, cunt. You've got no fucking idea!" And then she left.

I almost collapsed, my legs weak. My breathing all over the place, I struggled to get that under control while I rummaged under the counter for the front door keys. My agenda only had two things on it: lock the door and call J.

"Babe, I'm kinda busy right now," he answered with that impatient tone he sometimes used on me. And that just served to piss me off. Being pissed off I could handle. It was an emotion I welcomed any day over terror.

"Yeah, well, *babe*, I think you might want to stop what you're doing and listen the fuck up."

Yeah, fear had definitely left and anger had walked right on in, and settled itself down.

"What the fuck, Madison?" It was J's turn to get shitty.

"I've just had a visit from Mandy," I threw it out there, and waited for it to wrap itself around his head.

"Fuck!" he bellowed, and I had to hold the phone away from my ear for a moment. "Are you okay?" Even though his voice was still angry, I heard the softness for me in there, melting some of my anger away.

"Yeah, baby, but I need you. Can you come now?"

"I'm already on my way," he said, and the relief hit me like a gush of wind.

"Thank you," I breathed out, my anger dispersing with it.

We ended the call and I waited for him. My mind raced with crazy thoughts threaded with fear.

And then it hit me.

Fuck.

I needed a drink.

22

Jason

Fuck!

Scott, Griff and I arrived at Madison's work within half an hour of receiving her call, and she was nowhere to be found. The shop was locked and she didn't answer the door, so Scott had broken the lock. She wasn't there. And she wasn't answering her goddamn phone.

I raked my fingers through my hair. Where the fuck could she be?

And then Griff voiced what we were all thinking. "Do we think Mandy came back for her?"

"I'll fucking kill that cunt if she touches Madison!" I roared and turned to leave the empty shop.

"Brother, I'll kill her even if she doesn't," Scott promised me, and I nodded at him in silent agreement.

Scott pulled out his phone and called Marcus to break

the bad news to him. They came up with a plan of attack
and we began our search for Madison.

TWO HOURS LATER, we still hadn't located either of them.
Desperation was setting in and Scott was beyond a state of
rage. I didn't think he loved anyone as much as he loved
his sister.

We arrived back at the clubhouse to regroup. All the
boys were there. Madison meant so much to all of them,
and it was a sombre mood that permeated the room.

Marcus took control. "I want every fucking person tied
up with that bitch to be grilled. One of them has to know
where she is. Scott will coordinate," he directed, and then
left the room. I wasn't sure where or what he was doing,
and even though it was odd that he would leave us to do
this on our own, it wasn't my concern. Finding Madison
was my only priority.

I got my directions off Scott and headed out. My first
stop was only ten minutes from the clubhouse, and as I
pulled up, my phone started ringing.

It was Brooke. "Hey, sis," I answered, hoping she
was okay.

"J, are you with Madison today?" Nervousness laced
her voice.

Unease hit me in the gut. "No. She got a visit from
Nix's crazy sister, and now we can't find her. Why? Have
you heard something?"

"I think she might be at Hyde's."

"What?" I struggled to make the connection.

Brooke sighed. "J, I think she's been drinking. One of my friends just called me and suggested I get you down there to stop her.

Unease slid right through me and fury took its place.

"Thanks, I'm on my way now," I bit out and hung up.

∽

I WALKED through the doors of Hyde's pub ten minutes later. A combination of the struggle of watching Madison lose herself to alcohol years ago mixed with the burning anger and resentment I still held towards my alcoholic mother, meant that I lost it.

She sat at a table with some guy and a drink in front of her.

I saw red and stalked to where she sat. "What the fuck are you doing?" I yelled at her.

When she turned her face to look up at me, the conflict I saw in her eyes hit me in the gut. However, my anger and disappointment with her were too far gone to slow me down.

I met the dude's eyes. "Get the fuck out of here!" I roared. He shrugged and left. *Yeah, smart move, motherfucker.*

"I'm sorry." She shifted her gaze away from mine as she uttered the words.

"Have you had any yet?" I demanded, clenching my fists by my side.

She shook her head but refused to meet my eyes. "No,"

she whispered and I could hear the agony in her voice. And still I couldn't dial my disappointment back. Alcoholism was something I struggled to understand and I thought she'd moved past these kinds of setbacks.

I thought she was stronger.

I picked up the glass of alcohol and carried it to the bar. Depositing it there, I stalked back to Madison.

She finally turned her face to me. "Please don't be mad, J." Her eyes begged me in the same way her voice did.

I didn't want to be mad, but, shit, I couldn't stop the emotions as they rolled through me. Rubbing the back of my neck, I grit out, "It's time to go."

She stared at me for a long few moments and right when I thought she was about to say something, Scott rang. While I took his call and filled him in on where Madison was, she slid off her seat and walked outside without saying a word.

I followed her in silence. It was better that we didn't speak; with my conflicted thoughts, I wasn't sure I could be trusted not to say something we couldn't come back from.

23

MADISON

I WAITED FOR it.

Whatever he was going to say was nothing compared to what I was screaming at myself. I hated myself. Hated that I had let myself almost drink again.

The energy instantly changed when he entered the house. He seemed to be filled with rage and disappointment. It was the disappointment that pierced my heart the most. To have a loved one disappointed in you, was one of the worst feelings in the world. I wanted to run from him and never look back. Never have to experience the look he was giving me.

We stood there, watching each other for what felt like eternity. I crossed my arms, as if by doing so, I could shield myself from him. He clenched and unclenched his fists, and I noticed the muscles in his neck twitch.

Finally, he spoke. "Why?"

Out of all the things to ask an alcoholic, that was maybe the one thing we never wanted to be asked. For me, anyway. Because, it was the one question that I sometimes couldn't answer. Or maybe, it was the one question I didn't want to answer.

I sighed, and fell into the couch behind me, dropping my face into my hands.

"I asked you why!" His voice boomed throughout the room.

Shocked, I jumped in my seat. I looked up at him. "I don't know." My words were pathetic, and he knew it.

"That's not a fucking answer, Madison. Tell me why."

Fucked. I was fucked. The situation was fucked, and I wondered if J and I were fucked. Again.

Resentment at what was happening flared in me. I stood and came face to face with him. "Have you ever made a mistake in your life that you felt like you couldn't come back from?"

"Yes." That was all he said, but it was enough for me to run with.

"I don't know if I can come back from what we did to Rob," I admitted. Finally. It had taken me years to say those words.

He looked confused. "You haven't had a drink in over two years, and then today you want a drink because of Rob?"

I shook my head. "Today wasn't because of Rob directly, but can't you see, J? Everything bad that has happened since then has been because we killed him."

"I killed him. Not you. And I still don't see what you're saying."

"You only killed him because of me. And then, because of that, I started drinking. We broke up. I dated Nix. And the shit we're in now is because of all that!" I laid it all out for him. Why couldn't he see it?

"Babe, your thinking is fucked up. I get what you're saying, but it's fucked up. Everything in life has a consequence. If we all started analysing shit like you are, we'd all be screwed."

"Alcohol takes away the shittiness I feel in my soul about it all. I haven't felt like that for a long time, but Mandy brought it all back to me today. In answer to your question, that's why."

"Not fucking good enough, babe. You could have come to me, talked it through—"

I cut him off. He just didn't get it; he probably never would. "I don't want to talk about it, J! Talking doesn't solve anything; the problems won't go away just because we talk about it."

Pacing, he ran his hands madly through his hair. "I think you should go to bed. This is obviously not the right time for us to discuss this," he said.

My heart sunk and my shame almost swallowed me. I wanted desperately to help him understand but he was right – this wasn't the time to talk. We both needed some space and some time to calm down and get our thinking straight.

I nodded. "You're right," I agreed softly and with one last look at him, I turned and left the room.

Tomorrow was another day and hopefully he'd give me a chance then to explain myself.

I need him to understand.

Without his support, I wasn't sure how I'd move past this setback.

THE NEXT MORNING, I woke up alone. J didn't come to bed. My head pounded from the stress and my heart was bleeding. I didn't know where our argument had left us.

I showered and got ready for the day. I also wasn't sure if I still had a job since I had just left the shop in the middle of the afternoon. The house was so quiet, and I wondered if J had already left.

When I made it out to the kitchen, I found a note on the bench. J had left early, on club business. I felt a reprieve, if only for a short time. But it gave me the space I needed to get my head together, and start sorting through all the crap in there.

I had some toast for breakfast and guzzled some water. I also popped a few painkillers to try and ease the massive headache I had. Christ, what a mess I had gotten myself in. I resisted the urge to call Serena or Blake; they didn't need this shit dumped on them. I would deal with this myself.

My day took another dip in the crappy direction when I walked outside to go to work. Someone had slashed all the tyres on J's Jeep. Fuck! Not what we needed! I called for a taxi and then phoned a tyre shop to come and organise the replacement of all the tyres. J didn't need to be bothered with this; I would sort it out for him. He already had enough on his plate.

~

A COUPLE OF HOURS LATER, I was at work, my boss not even aware that I'd left early the previous day. She hadn't come in that morning, so I was able to get the shop in order so she never even realised anything was wrong. At last, something was going my way. My headache was starting to ease, so that was another positive to my morning. At that point, I needed to count all the positives; otherwise, I would drown in the negatives.

My senses went into overdrive when I heard the rumbling of a bike. *Shit. J.*

I took a peek outside, and sure enough, it was him. He cut the engine, yanked his helmet off, and strode into the shop.

"Do you care to tell me why there are men changing tyres on my Jeep?" he snapped.

I met his eyes, refusing to bow under his anger. "Oh, go to hell, J. I was trying to do you a favour."

"I appreciate that, but why didn't you call me?"

"I was trying to help you because I know you've got a lot on at the moment. You didn't need to be worried with anything else to take care of."

He took a deep breath, holding it in. Then he blew it out on a frustrated exhale. "That's a problem for me," he stated, his jaw clenching.

Oh, good God. What was his fucking problem? "Why?" I maintained my calm.

"Babe, we're together, are we not?"

"Yes, but—"

"No buts. We're together. So, when something like that happens, we handle it together."

My stomach fluttered, and want pooled there, leaving me stunned. "Okay," I half whispered.

"Good," he said, and then his features softened. "I've got a long day today, but I want us to talk tonight."

I nodded, the fight gone from me. "Yeah, baby."

He reached out and curved his arm around my waist, pulling me to him. "I love you," he murmured, and his lips met mine in a hard kiss.

"I love you, too."

I watched him go, my thoughts and feelings in turmoil. J had not reacted at all how I thought he would. A glimmer of hope peeked out; maybe there was a chance for us after all.

24

MADISON

J ARRIVED HOME after ten that night. I'd been sleeping on the couch on and off, waiting for him. He came into the house and headed straight into the bedroom. I waited silently for him to come back out; I had absolutely no idea where our conversation was headed.

"You've had dinner?" he said, as he came back into the lounge room.

"Yeah. I made you some if you haven't eaten."

He smiled at me. I let the gesture settle over me and wrap itself around my heart. If we were going to get anywhere, I would need to keep a hold of that. I feared we were in for another tense discussion.

"Thanks, baby. I ate with the boys, so I'll put it in the fridge for tomorrow," he said as he went to the kitchen to take care of it.

I got up and followed him, the need to be near him overwhelming. He turned to me when he heard me enter the kitchen behind him. I stepped into his space, and wrapped my arms around him, inhaling his scent and brushing his neck with my lips.

A groan escaped his lips, and his arms encircled me too. He bent to lay a kiss on my head, and then he murmured, "I was so worried about you yesterday, and relieved when I found out you were okay. But babe, you scared the fuck out of me by almost drinking."

I pulled away a little bit so that I could look into his eyes. "I'm so sorry. I think I scared myself too. I'm so ashamed," I admitted.

He reached his hand out to my chin, and held it gently, tenderly. "Don't be ashamed. Okay? You need to move past this and that won't help you. It was a bad day, and yeah, you didn't handle it the best. But babe, we all have days like that. It's how you handle it now, and the next time it happens, that counts. And, I need you to know I'm here for you. I want to be the person you turn to when shit gets real. Can you let me be that for you?"

The tears started falling and I was helpless to stop them. I nodded, struggling to speak. Finally, the words came. "I thought you were going to leave me," I said quietly.

Pain flashed in his eyes. "Fuck, babe. No, that thought hadn't even crossed my mind. Yeah, I was mad as hell at you, but this, what we've got here...this is for-fucking-ever. I love you no matter what you do. It's unconditional for me."

At those words, his promise, I sagged against him. He

would never know how much I needed to hear that. "Thank you."

"We're going to have a lot more fights. You know that, right?" he said.

I smiled. "Yeah, I've worked that out."

"So we need to agree right fucking now that this is forever. That we're on the same page here. Are you in this for the long haul?"

I touched my hand to his cheek and let it linger there. "Yes, I am. I love you. Unconditionally."

He bowed his head and breathed hard for a moment. Then he looked back up at me. The love I saw there smacked into me, leaving me winded. "You have no idea how much I needed to hear that," he said, his voice full of raw emotion.

"Oh, I think I might, baby. I needed it tonight too."

He took my hand and kissed it, softly. "We've got a lot more to talk through, but for now, I just want to take you to bed and show you how much I love you."

I smiled and let him lead me to the bedroom. As we walked, I peeled clothes off, leaving them throughout the house. When we made it to the bedroom, he turned and ran his gaze over my naked body. I watched as his eyes glazed over with desire, my nipples hardening under his stare.

He reached his hand out to trace a line from my lips, down my neck, and to my breast. As his fingers found my nipple, he brought his mouth down to meet it and licked and sucked my breasts, one at a time. His other hand came up, so that both of them were massaging my breasts, while his tongue drove me wild.

I moved my hands to lift his shirt over his head, and he

stopped what he was doing to allow this. Once it was off, I quickly reached to undo his jeans, and remove them too. My breathing picked up, and my fingers ached with a need to touch, to feel, and to show him how much I wanted him.

He stood before me, naked and beautiful. There wasn't anything about J's body I would change. I placed my hand on his chest, over his heart, and held it there while I focused my eyes on his. The invisible thread that held us together sizzled with desire and white hot lust. But tonight, it held something more; a burning love that had been buried under layers of doubt, guilt and hurt. Our love shined brightly; we had finally found our way through, and peeled away those layers by committing completely to each other. We had promised forever, and those words had exposed the raw love that existed between us.

J felt it too. I could see it in the way he looked at me. Hunger for this man engulfed me. I moved my hand up to curl around his neck, and pulled his mouth down to mine. Our kiss was deep and full of need. His hand snaked around my waist and pulled me to him. I moaned when his erection hit my body. God, I loved his cock.

"I need to taste you, baby. Need my tongue in that sweet pussy of yours," he murmured into my ear, while backing me up against the wall.

I didn't argue as he knelt in front of me and spread my legs. When his tongue hit my clit, I scrunched my fingers in his hair, and cried out with pleasure. He grunted his satisfaction, and slid his tongue down and into my pussy. Oh, holy fuck, it felt divine. His hands moved slowly up the backs of my legs until they hit my ass. He kneaded my bottom, while his tongue continued to lick and stroke my sex.

Pleasure moved through me until my whole body was alive with it. When he began to fuck me with his fingers, I knew it wouldn't be long until I came. The pleasure intensified and built, until it crashed all around me, and I came with his mouth wrapped around my pussy.

My hands still in his hair, I pulled him up to me, to kiss him. I needed his tongue in my mouth. And the taste of me in his mouth only made me want him more. I groaned into his mouth, and pushed my body closer into his. My arms wound tightly around him, fingers clawing his back. One leg was wrapped around one of his, and all of a sudden, he gripped my ass and lifted me, carrying me to the bed.

As I fell to the bed, he leaned over me and smiled. "Fuck, I love fucking you. But tonight I want to make love."

I shook my head, and trailed a finger down his chest. "No, baby. Fucking is our way of making love. I want you to fuck me." And with that, I reached down to his cock, gripped it hard and pulled him to me.

"Fuck!" he roared, and thrust in, hard, just the way I liked it.

A deliciously wicked grin flashed across his face, and then our lips were locked while he fucked me just like I'd asked him to.

25

MADISON

I STARTED GOING to regular AA meetings again. J insisted, but I had already decided it would be an important part of my life. I had fooled myself into believing I was better than everyone at those meetings; that somehow I didn't really need to be there. I was wrong.

It was a month after my near miss and things between J and I were good. I was worried though; there was something bothering him and he wasn't talking to me about it. He was sharing more with me and even though I sensed he still didn't tell me a lot, I knew he was trying, and that was all I could ask for. Strong relationships weren't built quickly; I knew it would take a lot of work, so I was being patient. And yet, I felt it in my gut that something wasn't quite right with him.

The club still hadn't found Mandy, so I guessed he was stressed about that. I'd brushed my concerns away for a few weeks, but that week he seemed even more preoccupied with whatever it was. He was being elusive, and there also seemed to be some tension between him and Scott.

It all came to a head on the Friday afternoon of that week. I was waiting for J at the clubhouse when Griff wandered into the bar and locked eyes on me. Now, there was a man who I wasn't quite sure what to make of. He'd been a member of Storm for about three years and I still knew nothing about him except that he liked to keep to himself. If I had to choose one word to describe him, it would be broody. I took in his appearance. He was tall with dark hair that was a little long, kind of like he just needed a good haircut, but I liked the ruggedness of it. He also always wore a five-o'clock shadow; another great feature as far as I was concerned. I liked a man who wasn't perfect looking and he definitely fit the bill. Griff was one of the only bikers I knew who wasn't covered in ink; well, ink that could be seen anyway. His tanned skin was clear of them on his arms, neck and hands. I had no idea if he had any on his legs as I had never seen them.

His green eyes penetrated mine, and I felt a little disloyal to J with the sensations he evoked in me. His voice was deep and commanding when he spoke, "Scott wants to see you in the office."

"And why couldn't Scott come and see me?" I asked.

"In the office now, Madison," his voice rumbled, and his hand slid around my back to guide me in the direction he wanted me to go.

I wanted to argue with him, but something about Griff told me not to bother. If it was at all possible, he seemed bossier than J, with an air about him that screamed not to challenge. So, I did what I was told and went to see Scott, with Griff close behind.

Scott was sitting at my father's desk when we found him, and he looked up with a frustrated look on his face. Putting his pen down, he motioned for me to sit. Griff closed the door behind us and stood next to my chair. My senses went into overdrive; something wasn't right here.

Scott finally spoke, "Are you up on what J's been doing this week?"

"I've got no idea what J does with his time when he's not with me," I answered truthfully.

"Fuck," Scott cursed and shot a look at Griff, who nodded and then exited the room.

Okay, I was really confused. "What's going on, Scott?"

He sighed and then gave me a hard look, like he was contemplating just how much to share with me. "I was hoping you could tell us because we sure as fuck don't know what he's doing."

"Spit the rest out, Scott. What are you hiding from me?"

"Shit, Madison, this is club business," he snapped, and paused for a moment, rubbing his chin and scowling at me before continuing, "We're pretty sure he's still out there looking for Mandy, even though we've told him to stop. Problem is, it's bringing heat to the club because that bitch is tied to a gang who don't much appreciate the way J is going about it. Seems he is harassing their members for information."

I decided it was time to back my man. "Why isn't the

club interested in finding her and dealing with her? That bitch threatened me."

"Again, club fucking business, but seems as though I know you won't let this go… she's dating one of the head guys of the gang. We take her out, and who fucking knows what will come of it. They don't mess around, and we don't need a war. J needs to be smart about this, but I think his head is all messed up with you."

"So you're happy to leave me a sitting target."

"No. We're watching you when J's not with you, making sure you're okay—"

I cut him off. "This sounds very fucking familiar, Scott. Reminiscent of what happened with Nix. Only this time, I'm not going to lay down and wait for her to come to me," I ranted at him before storming out of the office.

As I was leaving, I ran into my father. He looked tired, and there was something else there that I couldn't quite put my finger on.

"I heard your argument with Scott. There's more to this that you don't know, and I'm asking you to leave it be. And get J to leave it alone too." His words held a warning. I searched his eyes, his face, and then I realised what other emotion he was running on. Fear.

"What is it?" I asked, even though I was fairly sure he wouldn't tell me.

"Not going there with you, Madison. But leave it the fuck alone," he ordered harshly.

His words stung. I hated it when he spoke to me like that. I met his glare. "Sometimes, I fucking hate this club and your bullshit ways of hiding stuff," I spat.

He opened his mouth to say something, but my mother

caught both our eyes, and he went quiet. I was stunned at her appearance. Her face was stained with black mascara. There was also a red mark on her cheek; it looked like she'd been slapped. She had entered the room we were in, but when she saw us, she went to leave.

Christ, what was wrong with her? My mother never cried. And then, looking from her to my father, and noting the displeasure that crossed both their faces, I realised what was going on. Clarity hit me fair in the gut, and shock sliced through my heart.

I whipped my head around to face him. "You fucking hit her?" I almost screamed.

He shoved his face in mine, and snarled, "I said, leave it fucking be." And with that, he left me standing there, wondering what the hell was going on, and feeling like our lives were about to be tipped on their asses.

J.

I needed J. He wanted to be my go-to person, and at that moment, I needed him to be that.

26

MADISON

"**H**EY, BABE. WHAT'S up?" J answered his phone straight away.

Thank fuck.

"I need you, now."

He must have sensed the urgency in my voice. "What's wrong?" It was like he was on instant alert.

"Something's happened. Between Mum and Dad. It's bad, babe. Are you close to the clubhouse?"

"Fuck!" he swore. "I'm about ten minutes away. Sit tight. I won't be long."

"Okay. Thanks, baby."

We hung up and I threw my phone in my bag. My mother had left without saying anything to me, and there was no way I was staying inside with my father still there, so I waited outside for J.

He must have sped the rest of the way, because he

arrived within five minutes. When he went to cut the engine, I shook my head and indicated that I wanted to leave on his bike. I couldn't get out of there fast enough.

I hopped on, and wrapped my arms around his body, nestling my head against his back. He made me feel safe, and in that instant, my heart expanded with love for him. Over the past few months, we'd been navigating the hills and valleys of our relationship. Some of those roads had been rocky, and we had clung to each other. I knew in my gut that we were about to hit a really fucking rugged valley, and that the only way through would be to hold onto J for dear life.

"SCOTT'S SHITTY with you and wants to know what you've been up to this week. And my father told me to leave it alone and to get you to do the same. What's going on, J?" We'd made it home, and I was determined to get him to open up to me.

He ran his fingers through his hair, and looked pained. "Babe, this is stuff I don't want you mixed up in; stuff I don't want you worrying about."

"No. We're together. For the long haul, as you once put it. And I want to have your back, J. So, for me to do that, you've gotta start talking."

"Fuck," he muttered, and began pacing.

I stayed silent, waiting for him to continue. When he finally did start talking, he blew my world apart.

"I don't want to tell you this. Fuck." He sat on the

couch, pulling me down with him. One hand grasped mine, and the other cupped my cheek. His thumb grazed my lips, and then finally, he spoke. "Mandy is running with a gang involved in drugs, prostitution and armed robberies. There could be other stuff, but that's what I know of so far. They're the kind of motherfuckers you don't mess with, but she's in deep. She's been dating their leader, Blade, for the past year or so. He ran a smart operation but has been building his ranks up for a few years now. They're big enough now that no one really wants to challenge them. Even Black Deeds leave them alone."

He paused, so I said, "I got the impression from Scott and Dad that they don't want to either, and I find that hard to believe. Storm is strong enough to do it."

He nodded, and then said quietly, "There's another reason why your Dad doesn't want to take them on, babe. And I don't think you're going to like it."

I had no idea what it could be, and why I wouldn't like it. "What?"

He blew out a long breath before he continued. "Blade is your half-brother. He's Marcus's son."

The room spun and I struggled to breathe. "What... how? Shit, does my mum know?" My thoughts and words weren't coherent so I stopped talking.

"Your mother found out today, and I thought your father was going to tell you too—"

"Scott knows, doesn't he?" I interrupted him.

"Yeah, babe. He's known for a little while. I found out this week."

"Does my dad have anything to do with Blade?"

The look that crossed J's face could only be described as devastated. That was when I knew; that was the moment the love I had for my father crumbled in a bloody mess of lies and deceit.

"Yeah, babe," he said softly, pulling me into a hug.

I welcomed his arms, his warmth, and sank into his love. We stayed like that for awhile; he gently caressed my hair and pressed his lips to my head. He was my shelter from the storm.

Eventually, I pulled away and asked him to tell me the rest.

"Blade was born after Scott, before you. He's four years older than you. His mother has been your father's mistress ever since, although from what I understand, they have been on and off throughout those years. Blade is their only child, and your father has had a relationship with him all his life. Blade has given Marcus his word that Mandy won't come after you again. Apparently, he wasn't aware that she was mixed up in all of this. Marcus and Scott have agreed not to pursue her."

I tried to take all of that in. "And you? Are you going against their orders?"

"I don't trust that bitch, and I want her taken care of. I'm pissed off that Marcus and Scott have backed off."

As I listened to what he was saying, I realised that this was the first time he had been so open with me about club stuff. Amongst all the crap we had going on, this was my shining light. It was a pivotal moment in our relationship. I gently laid my palm against his cheek. "Thank you," I murmured.

He looked confused. "What for?"

I smiled at him. "For telling me all of that even though I know you didn't want to."

He covered my hand with his and squeezed it lightly. "You were right to push me. And you were right that I need to tell you what's going on. Thank you for being patient, baby."

"I need to go and see Mum," I said, torn because I wanted to see her but I also wanted to stay right here with J.

"I'll take you."

I kissed him and grabbed my bag before heading out. I was apprehensive about what we would find when we got to my parents' house, but at least I had J with me.

∼

MY MOTHER ANSWERED the door dressed in a bathrobe. So out of character for her.

"Madison," she simply said in greeting. Her face was all puffy and she looked like shit, but at least that ugly red welt from where my father had slapped her was gone.

We followed her inside and sat at the kitchen table. My father was noticeably absent. Thank God, because I think I may have punched him if he had been there.

"So, you've heard the wonderful news, I take it. You have another brother." I didn't fail to note the sarcasm.

"Mum, talk to me," I pleaded.

J stood up. "I'll leave so you girls can have a talk," he offered.

"Sit down, J. You're part of this family, and as far as

I'm concerned, there should be no fucking secrets anymore," my mother said.

"Did you know before today?" I asked her.

She sighed. "I always suspected your father was playing around." She shrugged. "It's what happens in that club. I chose to ignore it. But I had no clue he had a mistress and a child."

I didn't want to ask my next question, but I couldn't stop myself. "Is that the first time he hit you?"

The way her shoulders slumped, and the sad look that flitted across her face told me what I needed to know. J made a noise and I looked at him. His fists were clenched and he ground his jaw.

"How bad, Mum?" I was so mad at not only my father, but also at myself, for not noticing. I had lived in a happy little bubble that was actually just one big, fat fucking lie.

She sat in front of me, a picture of vulnerability. I watched as she pulled herself together and plastered the stoic look that I knew so well onto her face. "Not as bad as some women receive. And only when I really pushed him."

Oh, my God. I couldn't believe what I was hearing. "Are you leaving him?" It was almost a challenge, because I was fairly sure I knew what she had already decided to do.

"No, and I don't want to hear your opinion on it. Or Scott's." Her eyes pierced me with defiance, and I knew there was no point arguing with her. Sharon Cole was not a woman who listened to other's opinions. But under that mask she wore, I knew there were cracks and all I could hope was that one day she would come to her senses.

27

JASON

I T HAD BEEN three weeks since Madison had discovered her father was a lying, cheating piece of shit. I had watched her struggle with this, and the fact that her mother was staying with him. I had also watched her begin to deal with it. And I couldn't have been fucking happier about how she was doing that.

My girl kicked ass.

It was a tough fucking pill to swallow when you realised the father you adored wasn't perfect after all. I knew because I'd been there. That knowledge took a piece of your heart with it, and you couldn't get it back. Ever.

We'd spent the last three weeks laying low, doing our own thing, away from the club as much as possible. I turned up every day for work, but I stayed out of Marcus's way. I would have probably knocked the fucker out if I'd run into him. Madison hadn't seen or spoken to any of her family in the last three weeks. She needed time to work through it all in her head.

The one thing she hadn't done was turn to alcohol. Sure, she hit as many AA meetings as she could, but mainly, she turned to me. And that was just how I fucking liked it.

We were enjoying a lazy Sunday morning in bed when she stole my heart all over again. "I can't imagine my life without you, J. Those years we spent apart were some of the hardest years of my life, but I think we needed them. They gave me time to grow up, and become me. And this me is so much better than the old me. This me is in your corner all the way, baby, and won't leave you ever again."

I rolled so I was on top of her and pinned her arms above her head, holding them there with one hand, while I moved my other hand to her breast. I dipped my mouth to hers, and took the kiss I desperately needed.

Coming up for air, I grinned at her. "God, I fucking love you, woman."

"I love you, too, baby. But can you let my hands go? I need to touch you."

"Wasn't in my plans, sweetheart, but perhaps you can convince me with your dirty words."

She lifted her head off the bed to bring her mouth to my ear. As she spoke, her warm breath sent desire straight to my dick, and I was a fucking goner. I didn't even pay attention to her words; she could have whatever the fuck she wanted.

I let her hands go, and she pressed them both to my chest and pushed me so that I rolled onto my back. The smile playing on her lips was delicious, inviting; I couldn't wait to see what she had planned for those lips.

She straddled me, her wet pussy teasing my cock as she slowly ground herself against me. Oh, she was a fucking expert at teasing. She rested her palms against my chest and bent forward to trail kisses up my stomach, to my chest. When she reached my nipples, she took one in her mouth and slowly sucked it, and then did the same to the other. Her warm, wet tongue was heaven, and my cock screamed out for it too.

"Baby, I want you to suck my cock," I said huskily.

She lifted her head and met my eyes. Her mouth spread back into that delicious smile. Yeah, my girl loved my cock. And she was straight on it. Her lips wrapped around me and she sucked me in as far as she could take me, her tongue gliding along my shaft as she went. She continued to suck as her hands massaged my balls. I lifted my hips off the bed, and she moaned as I tried to push my cock even further into her mouth. Madison was skilled at sex, but her talents with her tongue and mouth were by far her best. And I couldn't fucking get enough.

Just as I felt like I was going to explode, she stopped what she was doing and moved quickly to position my dick at her pussy. I pushed my hips off the bed again and slammed into her. We both cried out at the same time, and the primal need to be on top of her took over. I flipped us and continued to thrust into her. Her legs and arms wrapped around me, and she held on while I fucked her.

Our lovemaking may have been wild and frenzied, but it was full of love and passion. Some people showed their love with gentle and tender moments; Madison and I only knew one speed in everything we did in life. And doing it all together, we fit together perfectly in our imperfect love.

Madison

I squealed in delight. "So, you're definitely coming this weekend?"

Serena giggled on the other end of the phone. "Yes, chica. This weekend. It's a date."

Finally! She was *finally* able to visit after not being able to make it since I had moved back. I missed her so much and I could hardly contain my happiness. We finished our conversation and I smiled to myself. I was giddy, and I didn't do giddy. But J and Serena had turned me today.

He and I had just had amazing sex. God, I loved his cock. And, yeah that made me feel giddy all over again. Fuck, I needed to rein this shit in. I heard him turn off the shower, so I headed towards the bedroom. I needed to lay my greedy eyes on his body again.

As I walked past the spare bedroom, I noticed the curtain blowing in the wind. Strange. We never opened that window. I went in and shut it. J must have opened it for some reason. Having dealt with the window, my mind wandered back to J. I was so in love with that man. Unconditionally. And it felt amazing.

I hit the bedroom and came to an abrupt and chilling

stop. Mandy was in the bedroom with a gun trained on J. My heart started beating hard and fast. My mouth went dry and my legs felt weak.

Fuck!

She was ranting crap at him. I could hardly make out her words; she was in a crazy state. Oh, my God, our lives were in her psychotic hands.

As soon as she saw me, she turned and pointed the gun at me.

"You're gonna die, bitch!" she screamed.

"Let J go and I'm all yours." I needed to know he would be safe. I couldn't bear to think he would die because of me.

"Madi—" he started to say, but she cut him off.

Swinging to look at him, she yelled, "Shut the fuck up!" and then she swung back to me, her gun slashing through the air every time she moved. "And, no, he's not fucking leaving!"

"Okay. Mandy—" I began, and now she cut me off. Turned out the bitch wasn't interested in anything we had to say.

"You fucking took my brother away from me." She jabbed the gun in my direction, and I prayed it didn't go off, while mentally filing through options to get us out of this shit. "He loved you, and you broke his fucking heart."

What the fuck? Nix didn't love anyone. He just liked to control them.

Suddenly there was another presence in the room. I looked around, and came face to face with the spitting image of my father.

Blade.

The air whooshed out of my lungs, and I felt unstable. It was not how I pictured meeting him for the first time. He must have noticed because he reached out to steady me.

His eyes left mine and focused on Mandy. "You need to put the fucking gun down, and step over here," he spoke, his voice cold and harsh.

It was like he had a hypnotic effect on her, because she instantly calmed, and I saw doubt shadow her face. Her hand that was holding her gun began to lower. Just when I thought we had her, J lunged at her, and she turned to him. Time slowed right down for the next few seconds. It was one of those instances where you knew what was going to happen, and although you needed to stop it, there just wasn't time.

The gun went off, and J dropped to the ground, blood everywhere.

"No!" I screamed, and fell to my knees, scrambling to get to him.

Blade tackled Mandy, and another gunshot sounded. I had no idea who shot whom, or what happened; I was totally focused on J and the blood soaking through his shirt.

Time passed in a blur.

Sirens sounded.

People came into the room, and took J away.

My father turned up.

Scott arrived.

People spoke to me.

I didn't remember any of it.

J was gone.

28

MADISON
Four months later

"SO, SIS, TELL me who all these people are," Blade said, handing me a barbequed sausage on bread.

I angled my head to look at him. He was a tall guy, and well built. His eyes were the same colour as our fathers, a gorgeous green. He had also inherited the olive skin and dark hair that my father had. I hadn't met his mother, and I wondered what he had been blessed with from her.

We'd been spending time getting to know each other since J and Mandy were shot. I hadn't wanted to, but he'd pushed the point. And Blade wasn't a man who didn't get his way. I was slowly learning that. Why did I have to be surrounded by men like that? Why couldn't I have just one man in my life who *I* could boss around?

I pointed out a couple of the guys and told him a little about each one. He surprised me with his desire to know me, and to be a part of my life. Scott was distant with him, and Blade didn't try to force a relationship there. Perhaps it would come one day. Who knew what was in store for any of us? That was something I had really learned this year.

"You okay? Coping with today, without him here?" he asked, watching me intently.

"I'll be okay. Don't worry about me," I said.

He slowly nodded, still watching me, taking it all in. He was an intense man. Sometimes I didn't know what to make of it.

"Honey, can you help me with the soft drinks for the kids?" my mother called.

I nodded. "I'll meet you in the kitchen in a minute."

It was a club family barbeque. Storm had been through a lot over the year, and the day was a get together to help bring everyone back together, to help the healing process and strengthen club ties. The fallout from what I liked to call the 'Mandy Incident' was bad. A lot of the boys hadn't supported Dad and Scott in their desire to back off on her, and there was some lingering resentment from that. It turned out that J wasn't the only one who had wanted her dealt with.

Time was slowly healing the wounds, and I had no doubt the boys would work it out eventually. What I had some doubt about was letting Blade into the fold. He had been spending time at the clubhouse, meeting some of the boys. I hadn't been so sure they would welcome him, but they had. Blade just seemed to have that effect on you.

I left him and wandered into the kitchen to find

Mum. She seemed to be doing okay recently. She and Dad were working on their marriage. Well, I took her word for it because I hadn't spent time with them together since discovering his infidelity and tendency to hit her. I hadn't spent any time at all with my father, and I wasn't sure when I would be able to bring myself to do that. I didn't hate him, but I was still really angry at him. And I was pretty sure that would take a long time to go away.

"Hey, Mum." I smiled at her as I entered the kitchen.

She looked up and smiled back. "Hey, honey. Are you having a nice time today?"

I nodded. "I miss him, though." My word came out on a whisper, tears threatening.

"I know, sweetheart. But he wouldn't want you to be sad that he's not here."

"Yeah," I agreed, "you're right. Come on, let's get these drinks to the kids." I needed to busy myself and keep my mind occupied. Otherwise, I would be thinking of J the whole time. Missing him.

We grabbed the large Esky that was full of drinks and carried it outside to the sheltered area where the kids were set up with party food.

A hush fell over the party and all eyes were on me. I looked at Mum, but she was just smiling at me.

And then I saw him. My face lit up and my heart beat faster in excitement.

J.

I ran to him, and he caught me in a huge hug.

"Fuck, baby, I've missed you," he breathed into my ear.

"I've missed you too, so much. I'm never letting my father send you on a trip ever fucking again. Okay?"

After J had recovered from being shot, he had confronted my father over the whole 'Mandy Incident', and it had ended with them having a huge punch up. And when I say huge, I mean fucking gigantic. I'd never seen anyone take on my father like that before. They had both ended up with broken bones; it hadn't been pretty. Dad was so angry at J afterwards that he had sent him on a two month road trip to sort out club stuff that needed sorting out. Really, I had no idea what club stuff needed sorting out, but J had gone and done his time. I think it was some sort of club bullshit where you just have to do what the President told you to do.

He chuckled. "Yeah, babe. You tell that to your father."

"I fucking will," I threatened.

"Shut up and kiss me, woman," he ordered, and I willingly complied.

It was the most amazing kiss ever; full of the love and desire we had for each other. When we pulled apart, his gaze fixed on mine with an intensity I felt in my toes. "I love you, Madison Cole, and I'm going to spend the rest of my life with you."

I cocked my head to the side. "I love you, too, J. But if that's a marriage proposal, you've gotta do better than that."

He threw back his head and laughed. God, it was good to hear that sound. When he finished laughing, his eyes met mine, and a thrill ran through me. "Mark my words, baby, we're getting married. I'll find a special way to ask you, but for now, you just need to know that my heart is yours. You're the love of my life, and I'm never, ever letting you go."

I sighed, content in the warmth of his love.

I loved this man with all my heart. He'd shown me that even though life could be a bitch, love could get us through any storm.

ALSO BY NINA LEVINE

Storm MC Series

Storm

Fierce

Blaze

Revive

Slay

Sassy Christmas

Illusive

Command

Havoc

Sydney Storm MC Series

Relent

Nitro's Torment

Devil's Vengeance

Hyde's Absolution

Alpha Bad Boy Series

Be The One

Steal My Breath

ACKNOWLEDGMENTS

Baby girl, you will never know how thankful I am to you for giving me the space and time to write this book. You are one amazing kid, and yeah, it's a damn shame that you aren't older and able to beta read for me because the instant feedback would have been awesome ;)

To my amazing family (and this includes those not related by blood because I think we've already established that you are indeed family), you all believed in me before I believed in me. And for that, there are absolutely no words to express my deepest thanks.

To my parents, have I ever told you how much I love you? Your support and encouragement in everything I've ever done has been unwavering. It has meant the world to me. Thank you. I love you both so very much. Dad, all the marketing talks we've had over the years paid off. Even when you thought I might not have been taking it in, I was. It was being filed for later use. And that time has finally come. You gave me a scare this year, but it pushed me into action. Mum, I know you've read *50 Shades* but still... try to forget that your daughter wrote this book while you are reading it ;)

To my DBFFF, you fucking rock! God, where does one start to even say thank you for everything you do and have ever done for me? *You* showed me what unconditional love looks like. We've been friends for over 20 years, and there were definitely times there where I thought you would walk away from our friendship; that I'd pushed you just that bit too far. You showed me that that isn't how it works. The one thing I would wish for every woman and girl is that they have a best friend like you; one who is in their corner no matter what. I seriously don't know what women do if they don't have a best friend. Oh, and babe...you can't fucking write a book in a day. Seriously dude, what were you thinking? SMH. NFP.

To my brother, I've loved the last couple of years, chatting with you nearly every morning while we worked out how to solve the world's problems. You're another believer in me, and I thank you so much for that. In particular, your support over the past few months has meant so much to me. You let me chat books, and plots, and HEAs, and marketing, and every fucking thing else with you. You must be sick of hearing about the self-publishing industry by now!

To SL, one of us is overdressed and it ain't me... I mean, really, who cares whether you're wearing panties, panties or undies?? Just get them the hell off! *You*, my friend, are a little bit of awesome sauce. I'm gonna put you in a book (in my head I am hearing Keith Urban sing 'put you in a song' while I type that).

NN, the day you walked into our shop was a good day, my beautiful friend. Never saw you coming, but you just snuck up on me and now I am so thankful to call you my friend. Thanks for your belief and support.

To my KICKASS street team, Levine's Ladies, you girls make my day every damn day! I love you all. And I couldn't have done this without any of you. Thank you all so very much for being a part of this. You will never know just what you all mean to me. xxx

To the *amazing* bloggers and authors who have supported me. You are all rock stars! Thank you for everything you do. There are so many, but I do want to just shout out to Jani Kay, Carmen Jenner, Hook Me Up Book Blog, Island Lovelies Book Club, Sassy Mum Book Blog, Sizzling Pages Romance Reviews, The Danish Bookaholic, Louisa's Reviews, Sticky Reads, Give Me Books, Book Addict Mumma, Totally Booked & Natasha Is A Book Junkie. I also want to say a huge thank you to the amazing Aussie authors who have welcomed me into their group, given me advice and shared my book on their pages. What a great little indie community we have in Australia.

ABOUT THE AUTHOR

Nina Levine

Dreamer.
Coffee Lover.
Gypsy at heart.

USA Today Bestselling author who writes about alpha men & the women they love.

When I'm not creating with words you will find me planning my next getaway, visiting somewhere new in the world, having a long conversation over coffee and cake with a friend, creating with paper or curled up with a good book and chocolate.

I've been writing since I was twelve. Weaving words together has always been a form of therapy for me especially during my harder times. These days I'm proud that my words help others just as much as they help me.

www.ninalevinebooks.com